CO

Skye Fargo knew Maisie Wilson was too tempting for anybody's good, from the moment she thrust her way into his life. She attracted trouble like honey drew flies, and this time it came in the form of a young Sioux warrior, lean as a whip, tough as rawhide, and mad as a hornet when the Trailsman stopped him from having his way with Maisie when she went dipping naked in a stream.

Fargo and the Sioux faced each other, knives in hands. The Sioux was fast—fast as a cat leaping forward, slicing back and forth with quick, flat blows. Trying to find a moment for a counter-thrust, Fargo's heel hit a piece of rock. Flat on his back, he could only feel the pain of the kick that slammed into his hand and sent his knife flying. Yet Fargo still had one weapon left. He met the Sioux's eyes with his own, as he taunted the brave in the redskin's own tongue, "Come . . . kill me."

**BE SURE TO READ THE
OTHER BOOKS IN THIS EXCITING
TRAILSMAN SERIES!**

THE TRAILSMAN

165

DAKOTA DEATH HOUSE

by

Jon Sharpe

A SIGNET BOOK

SIGNET
Published by the Penguin Group
Penguin Books USA Inc., 375 Hudson Street,
New York, New York 10014, U.S.A.
Penguin Books Ltd, 27 Wrights Lane,
London W8 5TZ, England
Penguin Books Australia Ltd, Ringwood,
Victoria, Australia
Penguin Books Canada Ltd, 10 Alcorn Avenue,
Toronto, Ontario, Canada M4V 3B2
Penguin Books (N.Z.) Ltd, 182–190 Wairau Road,
Auckland 10, New Zealand

Penguin Books Ltd, Registered Offices:
Harmondsworth, Middlesex, England

First published by Signet, an imprint of Dutton Signet,
a division of Penguin Books USA Inc.

First Printing, September, 1995
10 9 8 7 6 5 4 3 2 1

The first chapter of this book previously appeared in *Nez Perce Nightmare*,
the one hundred sixty-fourth volume in this series.

 REGISTERED TRADEMARK—MARCA REGISTRADA

Printed in the United States of America

The Trailsman

Beginnings . . . they bend the tree and they mark the man. Skye Fargo was born when he was eighteen. Terror was his midwife, vengeance his first cry. Killing spawned Skye Fargo, ruthless, cold-blooded murder. Out of the acrid smoke of gunpowder still hanging in the air, he rose, cried out a promise never forgotten.

The Trailsman they began to call him all across the West: searcher, scout, hunter, the man who could see where others only looked, his skills for hire but not his soul, the man who lived each day to the fullest, yet trailed each tomorrow. Skye Fargo, the Trailsman, and the seeker who could take the wildness of a land and the wanting of a woman and make them his own.

1861, the Dakota territory,
somewhere east of the Black Hills,
a land of prairie passion . . .

1

It was a new experience for him, the big man with the lake-blue eyes thought to himself. Not being shot at—that had happened too damn often. It was the pleasantly sharp taste of mustard on his lips and the feel of more of it spattering his face. Fargo had been holding the small crock in one hand when the bullet slammed into it to send the thick yellow condiment spraying in all directions. But that was only one of the dozen shots that flew across the saloon as he dived for cover under the table. The beef-and-cheese sandwich on rye that he was about to season also flew into the air in pieces as another bullet tore through it. A piece of beef slapped him across the cheek as Fargo hit the floor.

His eyes going to the doorway, he saw the girl twist her body as she fired off two more shots before vanishing from sight. But the image stayed in his mind: her dark blond hair and trim figure appearing in the doorway, blazing away with the Smith & Wesson seven-shot, single-action revolver. Her shots, all aimed at the six men at the nearby table, hurtled first into the older gray-haired man with the dark jacket. In a split second, he was slumped facedown on the table, red rivulets gushing from his forehead and chest. Another man sprawled in the next chair, his head back, his eyes staring lifelessly up at the ceiling. A third figure lay groaning on the floor. But the others had turned toward him, bringing their guns around. "Get the son of a bitch. He set us up for her," one yelled as he fired, others joining him in a volley of shots.

Fargo ducked behind the heavy table as the shots whizzed past him. Putting his shoulder to the thick, heavy round table, he set it on its edge. Staying down behind it, he rolled the table toward the doorway as he cartwheeled his body with it. The fusillade of bullets slammed into the thick top of the table, a few coming out the other side, and he realized that others had joined in the firing. But he had reached the doorway with the rolling table and he dived from the saloon, hit the ground, rolled, and came up on his feet. He was racing across the ground and vaulted onto the Ovaro as his pursuers pushed their way past the overturned table in the doorway. Their shots, fired in angry haste, all were far off the mark as Fargo put the Ovaro into a gallop.

He leaned from the saddle as he raced down the street, his eyes searching the ground. The street was covered with hoofprints going in every direction. The marks would have been an indecipherable jumble to most men, but the Trailsman read signs the way other men read a newspaper. After a hundred yards of searching he spied the hoofprints he sought, big prints made by a big horse and, more importantly, fresh and dug deep into the ground, the marks of a horse racing at a full gallop. He followed the prints and saw where, a quarter-mile beyond town, she had turned from the road to race into a long line of hawthorn. She was in too big a hurry to take time to cover her tracks, and he easily trailed her path. But she was slowing her headlong flight, he saw, the horse's stride shortening, and he found himself thinking about everything that had happened and how he came to be chasing a very attractive young woman with an obviously very big hate.

It had really begun in Mary Kelso's arms, two towns away. Not that Mary had any idea of what was going to happen. She was just trying to do someone a favor. That was in keeping with Mary. He had just enjoyed three days and nights of Mary Kelso's deep, pillowy breasts and the richness of her full-fleshed body. Mary always held some fifteen pounds too much on her, but she carried it well, excess poundage evenly distributed over a strong-boned body. His visit to Mary had been his first in four years and came when he'd finished a long, hot cattle trail for the Edmundson brothers back in the Nebraska territory. Mary had been as wonderfully warm as she always had, and together they turned the clock back to those times when he had helped her leave Missouri and a no-good man.

"The world's a funny place. I was just talking about you last week when here you come a-visiting," Mary said, sitting up in bed, her full breasts swaying.

"Why were you talking about me?" Fargo inquired.

"I often talk about you," Mary said with a dreamy little smile of reminiscence. "But in this case I talked about you with a gal I know who could use some help. I told her you were the best trailsman in the West."

"Thanks, but I've a job waiting up Montana way when I leave you," Fargo told her.

"She'd be on your way. Stop in and see her. She'll do her own explaining. Her name's Maisie Wilson. She did me some favors when I first came here. I'd like to do her one now," Mary said as she leaned forward and pressed her full breasts into his face.

"For me, for old time's sake," she murmured.

"For you, Mary," Fargo murmured with one red-brown nipple against his lips. Mary uttered a deep sigh of contentment and turned the clock back again.

That was how he had come to meet Maisie Wilson, four days later, following Mary's directions to the outskirts of a town named Redrock and a store that sold used harnesses and wagon gear. Mary had said nothing to prepare him for so strikingly attractive a young woman. He took in dark blond hair pulled back in a ponytail, a wide mouth, straight nose, and even features. Tan Levi's did nothing to hide a firm, well-modeled body with long legs and a small waist. A black-and-white-checkered shirt, open at the neck, showed high, tight breasts with a full curve to them. But it was her eyes that held him—they were brilliant, piercing blue, with an intensity unlike any eyes he had ever seen.

He introduced himself and her brows arched faintly as she sat down with him inside the small house. "Yes, Mary told me about you," she said. "And here you are. I guess it's time I got a run of luck."

"I'm afraid my stopping here was all Mary's idea. I've a job waiting for me in Montana. I don't see how I can be of help to you," Fargo said ruefully.

"Whatever they're offering you, I'll pay you double," Maisie Wilson said.

"That's mighty generous of you, but I've people waiting for me," Fargo said.

"At least hear me out, Fargo," Maisie Wilson said.

"I've come this far." Fargo shrugged, and the young woman leaned back in the wooden chair, firm, high breasts pushing the checkered shirt outward.

"I want you to find a house for me," she said, and

Fargo's brows lifted. "A strange request, I know, but a very strange and very rich man had it built. I'd guess you'd call him an eccentric. He died, and I have to find that house."

"Why?"

"There's something in it I've got to find," Maisie Wilson said.

"Well, Maisie, I'd guess anybody can find a house for you. This doesn't need me," Fargo said.

"Nobody's been able to find it up to now, and I can't wait any longer. I need your help and I'll pay top dollar for it," she said.

Fargo frowned. "What's so important in this house?"

"I'll talk about that when you agree to help me," Maisie Wilson said.

"Sorry," Fargo replied. "You'll get somebody to find the house for you."

Maisie Wilson's intense blue eyes narrowed a fraction. "You saying you won't help me?" she remarked.

"It's not for me," Fargo shrugged. "And I've another job waiting."

She didn't answer for a long moment, but he felt the thoughts whirling behind the piercing blue eyes, which stayed on him. Finally, when he'd begun to wonder if she was going to say anything more, she offered a shrug of her own and a half smile. "Well, you took the time to come see me. You deserve a good meal for that. The Redrock Saloon has one of the best beef-and-cheese sandwiches in the territory. Let me treat you to one," she said.

"That's real nice of you, and I am hungry," Fargo said.

"Then it's a deal. Besides, I'd like to talk to you some more," Maisie Wilson said and rose to stride from the little office. He followed her outside and saw her holding the reins of a big bay—at least seventeen hands high—with a white blaze. He watched the high, firm breasts sway in unison as she swung into the saddle with easy grace. "I'm hoping that after a good meal you might reconsider," she said, flashing a quick, bright smile, the piercing blue eyes softening for a moment.

He knew that his own smile was ruefully apologetic as he climbed onto the Ovaro and rode beside her into Redrock, which was a very ordinary town to all appearances. "Lived here long?" he asked the young woman.

"Grew up near here. My pa worked on a big spread a mile from town," she said. When they reached a dry goods store, she pulled the big bay to a halt and dismounted. "I've an errand to do. The saloon's only two streets down. Go on ahead of me and I'll be along in a minute," she said, started to turn, and paused. "Take my horse and drop his reins over the hitching rail, would you?" she added.

"Sure," Fargo agreed.

"Order for yourself, meanwhile, just in case I'm delayed. I'll be along in plenty of time to pay." She laughed and flashed the bright smile again.

"Your show," Fargo said as he moved on, pulling the big bay along with him. The horse went along with no balking, and when he reached the saloon, Fargo dismounted and dropped the horse's reins over the hitching rail. He tethered the Ovaro alongside the bay. He felt eyes on him and turned abruptly to see a cowhand staring at him from just outside the saloon door. Wearing a frown as he stared, the cowhand abruptly turned, sudden alarm on his face, and ran through the swinging door and into the saloon.

A furrow digging into his brow, Fargo went into the saloon and quickly found the cowhand bent over a round table, talking to five other men seated there. Fargo saw all of them turn to look at him as he entered the saloon;

one a gray-haired man wearing a dark jacket and a string tie, gave him a particularly piercing stare. Fargo moved on and took a seat a few tables away. He noticed the men were still tossing glances his way as they conversed in furtive whispers. A waitress in a white blouse and short black skirt came to his table, and Fargo ordered the beef-and-cheese sandwich and a bourbon. She brought the bourbon first, and Fargo had just taken a long pull of it when the cowhand approached him.

"What are you doing with Maisie Wilson's horse, mister?" the man asked brusquely.

Fargo felt apprehension instantly pushing at him. "Why do you want to know?" he asked.

"Brad Kelly wants to know," the man answered and flicked a glance to the table where the five men sat.

"Brad Kelly? He wearing the dark jacket?" Fargo questioned, and the cowhand nodded. "Why's he want to know?" Fargo asked, growing more cautious.

"It's important to him," the cowhand said.

"Why?" Fargo repeated.

"Because it is. I'm not sayin' anything more," the cowhand answered.

"Me, neither. Get lost," Fargo said. The cowhand's face was clouded with truculent hostility as he hurried back to the table, where the others exchanged more whispers as they again shot quick glances his way. The waitress returned to put the sandwich plate in front of him and a small crock beside it.

"Your mustard," she said and ambled away. That was when he picked up the crock of mustard and that was when Maisie Wilson appeared in the doorway, firing a furious, fatal fusillade.

The images all disappeared and he was once again riding through the forest, his eyes searching the ground as he trailed the big bay. He slowed as he saw the stream where Maisie Wilson had taken the horse, thinking to throw off any pursuit. But she was an amateur, riding her horse too fast, and Fargo quickly saw the water marks kicked up on the banks.

She had gone upstream, and he swung the Ovaro alongside the stream to make better time. He saw where she finally left the stream and began to double back in a wide circle. She had slowed, and he estimated he wasn't more than a few minutes behind her. The hawthorn began to thin, and he glimpsed her and the big bay as she neared the end of the trees. Overconfident, she never glanced back until she caught the sound of his horse. It was too late, then, as he came up behind her. Maisie Wilson had shown she had no compunctions about shooting, and he had the Colt in his hand when he drew alongside her. She reined to a halt, glancing at the Colt and then back at him, surprise coming into her intense blue eyes.

"You are good. I'm impressed," Maisie Wilson said.

"Don't be. You weren't hard to track. You've a lot to learn," Fargo said coldly and saw her eyes narrow at him. "I'll take the gun," he said. "Nice and slow."

"There's no need for that. I'm not going to shoot you," Maisie said.

"Damn right you're not. The gun, honey," he said. Her eyes went to the Colt in his hand and back to his face. Slowly, she lifted the Smith & Wesson from her holster and handed it to him. "You set me up," Fargo said, pushing the gun into his pocket.

"That's a bit strong." Maisie half shrugged.

"That's the goddamn truth," Fargo snapped. "You knew there'd be a lookout waiting outside the saloon and you knew he'd see you hitch your horse to the rail. You didn't want that, so you set me up to do it for you."

"You said you weren't going to help me. I decided to get some use out of you," Maisie said with icy honesty.

"I gave you the moment you needed to take them by surprise," Fargo said.

"It worked," Maisie replied.

"It sure did, and it put my neck on the line," Fargo said.

"I didn't expect they'd go shooting at you," she said.

"Why not? It was natural they'd figure I was in on it with you," Fargo returned angrily. "I saw a sheriff's office in town. I'm sure that's what he's thinking now."

"I don't care what Sheriff Ludlow thinks," Maisie Wilson said.

"Well, I do, and you're going to set him right," Fargo said. Her sharp blue eyes bored into him and she didn't answer. "You're going back with me and tell him I wasn't part of it."

"Hell I am. I'm not putting myself in jail," she said.

"And I'm not going to be hunted for something I didn't do," Fargo said. "You killed a man named Brad Kelly, and two others. I'm not being blamed for that."

"I had my reasons."

"Such as?" Fargo questioned.

"Brad Kelly killed my pa, only a few days ago. Now he's paid for it," Maisie said icily.

"You tell the sheriff that?" Fargo asked.

"No," she said.

"Why not?"

"He'd want proof and I couldn't give him that. Brad Kelly was alone with my pa when he did it."

"But you're sure he did it," Fargo pressed.

"I'm sure. He was the only one with any reason to do

17

it," Maisie said. "But there's knowing and there's proving." Fargo grunted grimly, aware of the truth in that. "You want to hear all of it? It'll take some telling," she said.

Fargo's lips stayed grim. "No, I don't aim to know any more about this. I just want to go my way," he said, determined to avoid any further involvement in what was plainly a not-so-simple situation. "Look, you've got to tell the sheriff your story. I'll see that he hears you out. I'll promise you that," Fargo offered.

"No. I know Ludlow. He won't take my word," Maisie said.

"You'll have to convince him. You don't have any choice, girl. I'm taking you back," Fargo said.

Her lips pushed out in a half pout. "That's not fair. All you care about is your own skin," she accused.

"I've gotten to like it," Fargo said, took her reins, and wrapped them around the Ovaro's saddle horn. "Just so you don't try anything foolish on the way back," he said. "Now keep your hands in front of you and let's ride."

Maisie Wilson's eyes held appraisal and accusation in their deep blue depths as she rode beside him in silence. Fargo found himself wrestling with his own thoughts as he led the way back. He wanted to be sympathetic, wanted to believe her story about avenging the death of her father. That would give reason and responsibility for her actions. While it wouldn't excuse her murderous spree, it would soften her motives. Yet she had gunned down three men and used him as a pawn in doing so without the slightest compunction, he reminded himself. She exuded an icy purpose that made it hard to find sympathy.

He flicked glances at her as they rode and saw no signs of softening in her face, no remorse, regret, and no hint of fear or uncertainty. She rode with an almost casual aplomb, he noted. Maisie Wilson was an unquestionably fascinating young woman. But then a diamondback could be fascinating, he thought to himself. He rode on with a steady pace. The day was beginning to draw to an end when he neared the town. She had ridden in complete silence the entire way. "Nothing to say?" he asked as the buildings of Redrock came into sight.

"All right—I shouldn't have used you the way I did," Maisie said, her tone tinged with annoyance more than remorse.

"So far so good," Fargo remarked.

"But I still need you. I'm more sure than ever after the way you trailed me so easily. Look, you help me find that house and I'll go to Sheriff Ludlow and tell him how I used you," Maisie offered.

"You're still putting the cart before the horse, honey. You tell him the truth first. My Ovaro is too easy to spot. I'm not about to be hunted by every bounty hunter and range rat. You talk first. It's the right thing for you to do," Fargo said.

"I know what's right for me to do," Maisie said and returned to her silence. Fargo led the way into Redrock, and when he drew to a halt in front of the sheriff's office, a man rushed out, a silver star pinned to his brown shirt. Fargo took in a man in his forties, with graying hair and a little too much paunch, but having a square face, determined chin, and vigorous stride. Sheriff Ludlow had already drawn his gun, Fargo saw, as the lawman stared first at Maisie, astonishment flooding his square face.

"I'll be damned," he breathed and glanced at Fargo. "You're the one that was with her."

"Name's Fargo . . . Skye Fargo. The young lady has something to say to you," Fargo said.

"Well, I've sure got something to say to her," the sheriff growled. "And you, too, mister. I'll take your guns before there's any talking." Fargo nodded. He had expected as much and handed over Maisie's gun and his own Colt. "Now let's get inside," Sheriff Ludlow ordered. Inside the building, Fargo saw a small office fronting three cells. The sheriff stepped back to an old desk where he put Maisie's gun and the Colt into a top drawer. Fargo saw his eyes go to Maisie, who continued to appear totally unflustered. "Talk," the sheriff said. "I hope you're not going to try and tell me you didn't shoot Brad Kelly and two of his men, because a saloonful of people saw you do it."

"No," Fargo cut in. "Maisie's going to tell you that I wasn't part of it. Then she has some other things to say."

Sheriff Ludlow's eyes stayed on Maisie. "That true?" he asked.

"No, that's what he wants me to say. He said he'd kill me if I didn't say that. He was part of it all the way. He even helped me plan it," Maisie said.

Fargo felt the wave of incredulity sweep over him. He stared at Maisie, finally finding his tongue. "You little bitch. You lying little bitch," he gasped.

Maisie turned her gaze on him with calm, almost aggrieved innocence, but he caught the moment's flash of triumph in the icy blue eyes. In fury, he started toward her, but the sheriff's voice interrupted. "Stay right there, mister," the sheriff said, and Fargo halted, unable to do anything more than glare in speechless fury at Maisie Wilson.

2

Still wrapped in surprise and fury, Fargo spun on the sheriff. "She's lying, goddammit," he said.

"Get back against that cell, mister," the sheriff said, his gun steady.

"I brought her back here," Fargo said as he moved against the bars of the cell. "I didn't do it so she'd put my neck deeper in a noose." He paused as he saw Sheriff Ludlow flick a glance at Maisie.

Her eyes met the sheriff's questioning glance with frowning earnestness. "He was going to kill me if I didn't come back with him and say he was innocent. He said if I did that he'd find a way to get me out. I had to go along or be shot. I was going to say what he wanted me to say, but when I saw you had the drop on him I decided to tell the truth."

Fighting off another wave of astonishment, Fargo peered at Maisie as she waited with absolute calm. She was condemning him yet making no attempt to explain herself. It made no damn sense, he swore silently. "Dammit, why are you doing this?" he flung at her. She turned on an enigmatic smile that might have been intriguingly charming under other circumstances. At the moment he could only find it infuriating. "What's it going to get you?" he asked.

"It's going to get me what I want," Maisie said smugly. Fargo stared at her, as bewildered as he was furious.

"I've had enough of this. Get in that cell, mister," the sheriff cut in. "Close the door behind you. I've the both of you and that'll do for now. I'll sort out the rest later." Fargo eyed the sheriff's six-gun and saw the man's finger curled tightly around the trigger. Cursing silently, he stepped into the cell and pulled the door closed behind him. He heard the latch snap shut as the sheriff motioned to Maisie with the gun. "You get yourself into the next cell, girl," the sheriff ordered. Maisie stepped into the cell and closed the barred door behind her.

Breathing a deep sigh, the sheriff stepped back from the cells, holstered his gun, and lighted the lamp as dusk began to close over the town. "My deputy will take over here while I pay Judge Conant a visit," he said.

Maisie straightened up at once. "When?" she asked, and Fargo caught the note of sudden alarm in the single word.

"Soon as it gets dark," the sheriff said. "The deputy takes the early night shift."

Fargo watched Maisie take three quick steps that brought her against the cell door. "Sheriff, I've something to tell you," she said to Ludlow. "But it's only for you to hear." She stayed pressed against the bars as the sheriff came to stand against the cell. She spoke in a whisper and the sheriff inclined his head forward, his forehead touching the outside of the bars. Fargo felt the furrow dig into his own brow as he saw Maisie's right hand reach into the back of her Levi's, down below the waist. When her hand came out the pistol was clutched in her fingers—a Remington four-barrel derringer—and she pressed the gun to the sheriff's temple. "Do exactly as I say or you're a dead man," she murmured just loudly enough for Fargo to hear. "Open the cell door with your key. Nice and slowly." She was reaching between the bars to keep the derringer against the man's temple. Fargo watched Sheriff Ludlow use his key to open the cell door.

"You're going to be sorry for this, Maisie Wilson," the man muttered.

"Not as sorry as you will be if you make a wrong move," replied Maisie, still keeping the little pistol against the sheriff's temple. "Now drop your gun on the floor," she said, and the man obeyed, very aware that only the touch of her finger was between him and death. "Kick it away," Maisie said as the sheriff's gun lay on the floor. He obeyed again. Moving with sudden quickness, Maisie swung the door open and darted out, the derringer trained on the sheriff. "Get in the cell, Sheriff," she ordered, and the man obeyed as the gun pointed at his head without the hint of a waver.

She pushed the cell door shut when the sheriff was inside the cell, put the derringer into her pocket, and hurried to the desk where she retrieved her Smith & Wesson. "What about me?" Fargo shouted after her as she made for the outside door. "You can't just leave me here after you've put my neck in the noose."

"Sorry, I want to be out of here before that deputy arrives," Maisie said and slipped from the building without a backward glance.

"Goddamn you, girl," Fargo flung after her as the door shut. He turned to see the sheriff glaring at him.

"You helped her. You deserve whatever you get," Ludlow said.

Fargo swore silently as the thin, double-edged throwing knife seemed to throb in its ankle holster. But using it on the sheriff wouldn't bring him his freedom—not unless he found a way to get close enough to the man. He was turning the thought in his mind when the sheriff moved further away from him and gripped the bars of the cell with both hands. Fargo's eyes were narrowed as thoughts of Maisic Wilson whirled through his mind. Had it been revenge for his refusing to help her? That seemed a stupid and self-defeating kind of revenge. It didn't fit a young woman who had plainly made all her moves with icy purpose. Yet he had no other explanation and he glanced back to the sheriff.

"It's dark now. You won't pick up her trail in the night," he said.

"I'll have a posse out come morning," Ludlow said.

"You won't find her, but I could," Fargo said. "Turn me loose and I'll bring her back to you."

"Sure you will," Ludlow said with a bitter laugh. "You must take me for a damn fool."

"What do you know about her?" Fargo asked.

"Maisie Wilson's always been a problem, always demanding things. She used to embarrass her pa by the way she pushed him into things," the sheriff said.

"She says Brad Kelly killed her pa."

"He did, but Brad Kelly said it was self-defense," the man answered.

"You buy that?" Fargo questioned.

"I wasn't there. I've no proof otherwise. But I know one thing: Maisie sure didn't gun down Brad Kelly in self-defense, and I've a dozen people who can swear to that," the sheriff said.

Fargo was going to say something more about motive and revenge when the door opened and a man entered, young and earnest with a deputy's badge on his shirt. He halted and astonishment flooded his face as he stared at Sheriff Ludlow inside the cell. "What're you doin' in there, Sheriff?" he asked.

"Just open the goddamn door. I'll explain later. The extra keys are in the desk," the sheriff thundered, and the younger man hurried to the desk. He returned with the heavy key ring and opened the cell door. He nodded toward Fargo as Ludlow stepped from the cell door.

"Him, too?" he asked.

"Shit, no," the sheriff roared and turned to Fargo. "I'll bring her in when I catch up to her. Meanwhile, I've got you and that'll have to do. I may have to hang you separately, which won't bother me any." He spun on the young deputy. "I don't want you in here with him, Willie, even if he is behind bars. They're a tricky pair. You stand guard outside until I get back from seeing the judge."

"Whatever you say, Sheriff," the deputy said and followed Ludlow out of the building. The outside door slammed shut and Fargo stepped back and for the first time surveyed his surroundings. The cell held a cot, a toilet bucket, and a small, barred window high in the rear wall let in air. Fargo let a deep sigh escape him. The throwing knife was of no value against steel bars. He'd have to bide his time and wait for a chance to use it. He'd have but one chance. He had to make it the right one, he realized. He lay down on the narrow cot and stretched out, hands behind his head. He closed his eyes and once more cursed the unexplainable enigma that was Maisie Wilson. She had run and left him to be hung and her last words to him whirled through his mind.

It'll get me what I want, she had said in answer to his question. Revenge, was that the whole of it? He had refused to help her and she'd wanted revenge for that? He grimaced at the explanation. Yet she had killed Brad Kelly out of revenge. Was she a young woman obsessed with revenge? He had to admit the real possibility, and yet her icy purpose seemed too calculated for something as simple as revenge. He was still thinking about Maisie Wilson when the sound came, snapping his eyes open. He swung long legs from the cot and it came again, from the barred window at the rear of the cell.

Stretching on tiptoe, he reached the window and peered into the darkness as a pebble bounced from one of the bars. "Over here," he heard the whisper.

"Jesus," Fargo breathed as he made out the slender figure standing beside the big bay. "What are you doing here?" he asked in astonishment.

"Giving you a second chance," Maisie Wilson said. "I need your help. My offer still stands. You help me find that house and I'll get you out of there."

He stared at her as the realization swept over him, all she had done suddenly falling into place. "You were planning this all the way back," he said, unable to keep the awe from his voice. "Everything you said, everything you did, was aimed at this moment, to get what you wanted, me to help you."

"That's right," she said. "I had to get away from the sheriff and put you where all you have left is one choice."

"I'll be damned," Fargo murmured as he found himself once more grudgingly admiring her unswerving determination.

"You refused to help me. Now you've a last chance to change your mind. It's help me, or the sheriff's noose. Ludlow will need to hang somebody to save face. He'll use you," Maisie said.

Knowing the truth of her words, he fastened a narrow glance on her. "What if I agree to help you and then hightail it?" he asked.

"You won't do that. You're not that kind. You agree and you'll stay with it to the end," she said. "You read trails. I read people." He uttered a wry grunt. She was right, of course, wisdom born out of instinct. "Your call," Maisie said, her voice hardening. "Time's getting short."

"One condition," Fargo said. "You tell me everything, important, unimportant. Whatever I ask, you answer. Whatever you know, you tell me . . . all of it."

"Agreed," Maisie said. "You just be ready to leave." He watched her move from his line of vision, pulling the big bay along with her. Moving from the barred window, he returned to the front of the cell, still awestruck at Maisie's undeviating purposefulness. It had never been simply revenge. It had always been her need to have his help. She had moved with quick-minded resourcefulness to get her way. Maisie Wilson was very definitely not to be underestimated. She had decided to take revenge for her father's death and nothing had stopped her in that, either. He was still thinking about Maisie when the front door opened and the deputy entered, Maisie right behind him with her revolver pushed into his back.

When she pushed the young man into the adjoining cell, Fargo saw that she had the keys to his cell in her hand. She opened the door and he stepped out and strode to the desk, retrieved his Colt, and kept the gun in his hand. "Sheriff Ludlow's not gonna like that," the deputy said from his cell. "It's gonna look worse for you, for both of you."

"You tell the sheriff we're all upset about that, Willie," Maisie tossed back as she kept the cell keys and hurried from the building. Outside, Fargo saw the big bay waiting and he holstered the Colt as three figures passed. "Your horse is in the town stable," Maisie said. "We'll just stroll over there nice and casual." He nodded and walked beside her as she led the bay down the main street in the night darkness, edging down an alley to avoid the stream of light and the crowd in front of the saloon.

The town stable was at the far end of Redrock, and a young stableboy appeared when they reached it. "Come for that Ovaro you have here," Fargo said.

"That horse is in Sheriff Ludlow's custody," the boy said.

"You going to stand in for the sheriff, sonny?" Fargo asked and rested one hand on the butt of the Colt.

"No, sir," the stableboy said, swallowing hard. "He's in the corner stall."

"Smart answer," Fargo said as he strode past the boy, found the Ovaro with the saddle still on him, and swung onto the horse. He guided the horse toward the door, where Maisie waited beside the bay. She was about to swing into the saddle when the shouts and the sound of running feet erupted in the night.

"Ludlow came back and found Willie," she said.

"He's got himself some help and he's on his way here," Fargo said. "He figured I'd come for my horse." He dismounted and drew the Colt as he shot a glance at the stableboy. "Find yourself a spot to hide back in the stable," he said. "There are going to be a lot of wild bullets."

"Yes, sir," the stableboy said as he ran. Fargo beckoned to Maisie as he led the Ovaro deeper into the stable and dropped to one knee. "We stay quiet, let them come to the door," Fargo said. "Then we lay down a volley, hit the saddle, and take off." She nodded as she took up a spot a half-dozen yards from where he waited. "Shoot

28

low. I don't fancy killing the town sheriff or his deputies. I just want out of here," Fargo said and raised the Colt as he saw the half-dozen figures running toward the stable, Sheriff Ludlow in the forefront.

He waited, watched as Ludlow and the others slowed when they neared the open stable doors, and saw the sheriff's deputy rush forward. Fargo took aim and barked his command to Maisie. "Fire," he said, and Willie went down at once with a cry of pain. Fargo heard Maisie shooting as he swung the Colt and caught the sheriff as the man tried to whirl away.

"Jesus, I'm shot," Ludlow bellowed. "My leg." Others were cursing in pain as Fargo and Maisie emptied their guns and Fargo rose to his feet.

"Let's go," he said. "Stay low in the saddle." He swung onto the Ovaro and raced from the stable, glanced back to see Maisie only a dozen feet behind. Their attackers were rolling on the ground in pain, but someone got off a few wild shots as the two horses raced into the dark streets. Fargo swerved through an alleyway between buildings and sent the Ovaro along the rear side of the town and up a low incline. He was beyond Redrock in minutes, Maisie alongside him. It had gone well, better than he'd expected, but he kept a fast pace until they were into the low hills. They reached a small stream where he drew to a halt and swung from the saddle. Under an almost full moon, Maisie's firm figure gracefully climbed from the big bay and she faced him, a tiny smile edging her even-featured face. Even in the moonlight, the intense ice-blue eyes crackled.

"Talk," Fargo said almost harshly. "The sheriff said Brad Kelly killed your pa in self-defense."

"Of course. That's what Brad Kelly told him," Maisie

said. "Pa went to Brad Kelly's place to talk to him, and Kelly killed him."

"Why?"

"Over the will, of course," Maisie said.

"What will?" Fargo queried.

"Davis Kendrick's will," Maisie said, and Fargo's lips pursed as he spied a flat stump and lowered himself down on it.

"Let's start from the beginning," he said. "Who's Davis Kendrick and how does he fit in?"

Maisie settled herself atop a half-rotted log, leaned back, and her firm, high breasts drew the shirt taut. "My pa and Brad Kelly worked for Davis Kendrick. You might say they were comanagers of all Kendrick's property just north of here."

"What kind of property?" Fargo interjected.

"Davis Kendrick was a very rich and very strange man. His property has a thousand acres of prime cattle and farm land, another few hundred acres of gold mine land. He never married, but he did keep women from time to time. They'd come, stay with him, and then suddenly vanish. He always said they'd gone their way with a nice bit of cash. Then one day Davis Kendrick took sick and up and died soon after. But before he died he said he had left a will, leaving all his property to one of his comanagers."

"Your pa or Brad Kelly," Fargo said, and Maisie nodded. "Both of them were sure they had been left everything in the will, I take it."

"That's right, but he left everything to my pa, Bob Wilson," Maisie said.

"What makes you so sure of that?" Fargo questioned.

"There are a lot of ways to know things. My pa and Brad Kelly each managed half of Davis Kendrick's property, including the mine. But Kendrick always favored the way my pa did things. Everybody knew it. Brad Kelly killing him was proof," Maisie said.

"How's that?" Fargo pressed.

Maisie's blue eyes turned chiding. "He did it so Pa wouldn't find the will and prove it," she said. "With Pa dead he'd have more time to look for the will and destroy it. That's why I've got to find that will to prove Pa was the one named in it."

"Davis Kendrick had a place on his property. Maybe that's where the will is," Fargo suggested.

"No. That place was searched by everyone, including my pa. The will's not there. Brad Kelly had three brothers in Oklahoma. They'll be on their way here to finish what their brother started, find the will, and now find me," Maisie said.

"What about this house you want me to find? Where does that fit in?" Fargo asked.

"Davis Kendrick had it built. He went off all by himself with a hired crew, all imported Italian craftsmen, to build it. It was one of the strange, secretive things he did. He never told anyone where it was or anything about it. He'd sneak off by night and spend weeks there."

"Which means it could be anywhere." Fargo frowned.

"No. Pa saw him load his packhorse one time and calculated he had supplies to travel north to a point east of the Black Hills on the way to the badlands," Maisie said.

Fargo's face grew taut. "That's still a hell of a lot of territory, and it's also smack in the middle of all kinds of Sioux tribes—the Sautee, Teton, and Yanktonai, to name just three," he said. "This house worth your scalp?"

"I'm counting on you to find the house and keep my scalp in one piece," Maisie said.

"I'm a trailsman, not a magician," Fargo grunted. "And you're sure this will is in that house he had built?"

"It has to be," Maisie said, and Fargo's eyes moved over her firm, compact figure and went to the big bay standing nearby.

"You better have more gear than what you've with you," he said.

"I do," Maisie said.

"At your place?"

"No. We had a house on Kendrick's property, as did Brad Kelly, but I left our place after Pa was murdered. I was afraid to stay and I set up somewhere else," Maisie said.

Fargo rose and pulled himself onto the Ovaro. "Let's get your things," he said.

"We won't be traveling alone," Maisie said as she climbed onto the bay.

Fargo raised one brow. "Meaning exactly what?" he asked.

"I hired some help before you came on the scene. They'll be valuable to us," she said.

"I'll be making that judgment," Fargo said, then grew uneasy at Maisie's silence. She gave no answer as she moved her horse west. He swung in beside her and enjoyed watching her handle the horse. She rode with easy assurance, thighs tight inside the Levi's, breasts swaying gently in unison, everything about her contained and controlled. The flesh follows the spirit, he thought silently, and stayed alongside her as she moved through narrow pathways in a stand of box elder. The moon had passed the midnight sky when Maisie turned west across an expanse of wheat grass, and as she finally slowed,

Fargo saw the three small tents that had been erected in a half-circle against a dozen hawthorns.

Two men holding Hawken plains rifles stepped forward and Maisie quickly called out. The men lowered their rifles at her voice and she drew to a halt and swung to the ground. Two more men appeared and Fargo dismounted as Maisie stepped before the men, gesturing with one hand to the big man at her side. "This is Skye Fargo. I've taken him on to find the house," she said.

"Where's that leave us?" the tallest one asked Maisie, a slight lisp in his speech.

"Same place as before. I want you boys with me," Maisie said. "But we'll all be taking trail orders from him."

Fargo saw the four men peer at him, uncertain sullenness in their faces. His experienced eyes took their measure in one quick glance: small-time hired hands, men who lived for the dollar, never anything more, men with guarded eyes and cracked-leather gun belts. Maisie gestured to the tallest one. "Fargo, this is Ken Kinnet. Next to him is Eddie Ray," she said. Kinnet had a tall, thin, straight figure and a slightly cadaverous face with deep-set eyes. Eddie Ray was burly with a square head and thick, fleshy lips that made him look not unlike a carp out of water. "Tommy Farkas and Josh Whitman," she finished. Farkas sported a thick head of unruly black hair, while Josh Whitman had more skin than hair on his head and lips stained yellow with tobacco juice.

"We'll talk more in the morning. Right now I think we'd all best get some sleep," Maisie said, and the four men turned away at once. Fargo was about to move toward the Ovaro when he saw the flap of the center tent open and a figure step out. The woman had long, dark blond hair that fell almost to her waist but did little to hide a very full figure inside a light blue nightdress. He took in deep breasts and a very round rear, a soft figure fashioned of curves that flowed into each other. He saw a pretty face, round-cheeked, a short nose, and lips so full they seemed to edge a pout. He felt a moment almost of shock as Maisie spoke. "My little sister, Marcy," she said. Fargo felt himself staring at Marcy Wilson, a young woman thoroughly different physically than Maisie, perhaps most of all in the smoldering dark brown eyes. Only the dark blond hair color was the same, and even that seemed different with the long, thick, full way it was worn.

"Hello, Marcy," Fargo said. The smoldering eyes stared back for a long moment, and then she turned wordlessly and disappeared back into the tent.

"She always that friendly?" Fargo asked Maisie.

"Marcy's got her problems, but she'll do what I say," Maisie answered. "Good night, Fargo."

"I take it I'm being dismissed," Fargo said with a smile.

"I'm tired. You've anything to say?" Maisie queried.

"Nothing that can't wait till morning," Fargo said, and Maisie stepped into the tent at the left.

Fargo took down his bedroll, went into the hawthorns, and slept quickly, waking only when dawn filtered through the foliage. He had washed and dressed when he saw Marcy step from the center tent. Still wearing the light nightdress, she brushed her hair with long, slow strokes. Fargo watched her breasts rise and fall rhythmically as she pulled the brush through her hair. The nightdress pressed against her body with each pull of the brush, outlining her thighs and the slight convex curve of her belly. She was all ripeness, he decided, hardly the image of a "little sister."

She turned suddenly, perhaps feeling his gaze on her,

and stopped brushing her hair as she faced him. "Didn't mean to interrupt. Don't stop," Fargo said.

"I'm finished," Marcy said, dark brown eyes moving over him.

"You can talk." Fargo half smiled.

"When I've a mind to," Marcy said flatly. Her eyes continued to appraise him with a penetrating examination. "You look like you might have a brain. How'd Maisie get you into this?" she asked.

"I'll let her tell you," Fargo answered.

"You afraid to?" Marcy queried. "She have you under her thumb already?"

He smiled at the sneer in Marcy's tone. "I'm not under anybody's thumb. I don't know that it's my place to tell you," he said.

Marcy's full lips stayed in their half sneer, half pout. "You think you know your place here?" she asked. "You're fooling yourself," she snorted, answering her own question. He watched her turn and walk into the tent, her round, full rear swaying under the nightdress. The four hired hands appeared, one holding a coffeepot, as Maisie stepped from her tent, dressed in Levi's and a brown shirt. She moved briskly and saw that Fargo received a tin cup of coffee and regarded him between sips from her own cup.

"We'll be ready to ride soon as the boys take down the tents," she said. Marcy appeared in a riding skirt and a white blouse that clung to the fullness of her deep breasts. Fargo saw the devouring glance Eddie Ray immediately fastened on her, and he motioned to Maisie as he moved to one side.

"I'm not happy," he muttered to Maisie. "You didn't tell me there'd be five more people going along."

35

"The more we are, the safer we'll be," she said.

"No," Fargo said tersely. "We'll have to sneak our way past the Sioux. There are only two ways to do that—one or two riders threading their way through, or a force of fifty guns. You don't have either. You've too many and not enough."

"What do you want me to do?" Maisie asked.

"Put Marcy somewhere safe and get rid of your hired hands. Then maybe you and I can get through," Fargo answered.

"No. The men go with us. They're important to me. They'll come in very handy," Maisie said.

"By getting us all scalped?"

Maisie's intense blue eyes took on a quiet implacability. "I'm counting on you to see that doesn't happen," she said.

"Don't," Fargo grunted, but Maisie's face remained set. It was more than stubbornness, he thought silently. He had already learned that Maisie had her own very good reasons for everything she did. He'd bring up the subject again, he promised himself, and turned away. The tents were taken down, folded, and put onto one of the packhorses. Fargo's lips were a thin line as he surveyed the scene. Marcy rode a solid quarter horse; the four hands were on nags as ordinary as they were. He counted again: Maisie, Marcy, the four hands—seven counting himself. Too many, too goddamn many, he knew.

He waved and started north with a silent curse on his lips.

3

The sun grew hot and Fargo slowed the pace and halted at every stream that wandered across his path. He was aware of Eddie Ray's eyes on Marcy. She was plainly oblivious to his covetous stares, too absorbed in her own silent, pouty sullenness. But Fargo had seen more than enough and he left the others behind as he rode on. The land remained mostly flat, long stretches of wheat grass grown so tall it reached the saddle of the Ovaro. He rode in a wide circle, his gaze scanning the terrain, before finally returning to meet the others as the day neared a close. He took Maisie aside after a supper of beans and dried-beef strips.

"I don't like the way Eddie Ray is eyeing Marcy. I'd say give him his walking papers," Fargo told her.

"Eddie Ray is the kind who ogles every woman. He's harmless. I'm not getting rid of anyone, Fargo," Maisie said.

Fargo gave her a probing glance. "What if you're wrong about him?"

"I'm not," Maisie snapped.

"Doesn't seem you care much about what happens to little sister Marcy," Fargo said tightly.

Maisie's sharp blue eyes flashed. "I'm doing enough

37

for her, so you let me worry about Marcy," she said. She strode away, set up one of the tents, and disappeared inside it. He saw Marcy curl up outside it with a blanket, the sullen half pout still on her round-cheeked face. Fargo had started to take his bedroll off by himself when he saw a figure standing to one side of a bush, watching Marcy. Fargo stayed and finally the figure turned away and a shaft of moonlight flashed on Eddie Ray's face.

Fargo set his bedroll down not far from Marcy, convinced that the man was far from harmless, and drew sleep around himself. But nothing woke him during the night, save the distant howls of timber wolves. When morning came, he woke to see Marcy on her side, the nightdress slipped down from one beautifully rounded shoulder. Fargo rose and dressed as Marcy woke and rose with lanquid gracefulness to step into the tent. When she emerged, dressed, Maisie came with her, and once again he was struck by how very different they were from one another. As Maisie had Ken Kinnet take down the tent, Fargo paused beside her. "I expect Brad Kelly's brothers have arrived by now and have gotten a posse together," he said.

"Probably," Maisie agreed.

"After a few hours of hard searching they'll have picked up our trail," Fargo said.

"You expect they'll be catching up soon?" Maisie asked.

"Not this soon. That's why I've pushed through wheat grass. It's tall and it springs back very quickly. It won't leave any easy trail to follow, and I want to stay in it as long as we can," Fargo said.

"Whatever you say," Maisie agreed.

"Let's make it as hard as we can for them. Don't ride

bunched together and don't ride single file. Ride spread out, a couple dozen yards between each of you," Fargo ordered.

"I'll ride at the far end," Marcy said.

"You'll ride near me," Maisie said, her tone sharp.

Marcy turned a disdainful glance at her. "Get off it. Where am I going to go?" she said.

"You ride near me," Maisie repeated coldly, and Fargo wheeled the Ovaro in a half-circle.

"I'll find you later. Head due north," he said and put the horse into a trot. He knew his lips were tight as he rode away and he vowed to take Marcy aside when he returned. He didn't like surprises, and Marcy's sullen hostility held the seeds of unexpected problems. Again, he sent the Ovaro into a wide circle that carried him beyond the wheat grass by midafternoon. He slowed to scan the shorter prairie buffalo grass. His eyes swept the horizon in every direction as he rode, aware he hadn't gone far enough yet to search for the house. But he looked for a wash or a draw or a thick stand of timber.

He saw only a few thin stands of red cedar and cursed the land that afforded little cover and less protection. His search found no draws or washes, nor any signs of unshod pony prints. By the day's end he circled back and met up with the others as they reached the end of the wheat grass. They were keeping separate, he saw with satisfaction, and he waved them forward as he led the way to a small cluster of shadbush. Maisie quickly put her tent up, and Ken Kinnet took a pack of beef strips from one of the packhorses and heated them over a small fire. Marcy sat off by herself, but Fargo saw Eddie Ray's eyes continue to stay on her. When the meal ended,

Fargo made his way to Marcy, who watched him approach with her smoldering eyes.

"I want to talk," he said.

"I don't," Marcy returned flatly.

"But you will. You've a mighty big bur under your saddle. I want to know what it is before it explodes in my face," Fargo said.

"It's between Maisie and me. It's not your concern," Marcy said sullenly.

"Now it is. Anything that affects this operation is my concern. Now, honey, you talk to me," Fargo said, his voice hardening.

Marcy was silent for a moment, but finally answered. "I don't want to be here," she said.

"Why not?"

"I've some money in a bank account. I wanted to take it and leave, but I can't get at it till I'm eighteen. That's another four months. I don't care about Davis Kendrick's mines or his property. I don't care who he left it to. It never made him happy," Marcy said.

"Your pa cared," Fargo said.

"Maisie was behind that. She was always the one who pushed Pa about the will. She's still pushing, even after he's dead," Marcy said and paused to fasten Fargo with a long, appraising glance. "You don't look like a fool. Why don't you just take off?" she questioned.

"I made a bargain," Fargo said.

"One Maisie set up, I'll bet," Marcy sniffed.

Fargo allowed a wry snort at her accuracy. "It's still a bargain," he said.

"She won't be grateful, if that's what you're thinking," Marcy said. "Maisie's never grateful."

"That's not what I'm thinking," Fargo said.

"Take off and I'll go with you. I'd be grateful," Marcy said. "I'm ready to be grateful to the right person for the right thing."

Fargo smiled as his eyes moved over the throbbing ripeness of her that fairly radiated from her full figure. "I'm sure of that," he said. "But I made a bargain. I gave my word. I'll keep it."

Marcy gave a disdainful sniff. "Then you're a fool on a fool's errand," she said. "You'll have to be pure lucky to find that house."

"Maybe not. I've an old friend, Dusty Smith. He might well have some word for me, if he's still alive and in the same place," Fargo said. "But that brings me back to you. You're here, like it or not. Make the best of it. I don't want to be worrying over what fool stunt you might pull because you're nursing your own grudges. I won't be standing for any problems from you."

"Strong words," Marcy said.

"Let's put it this way. I can be a real friend or a real enemy. That'll be your call," Fargo said. Marcy's sullen half pout remained as she turned away, but he saw the tiny furrow of thought touch her brow. He left her, took down his bedroll, and moved to one side of the camp—yet close enough to keep Marcy and the tent in his line of vision. He started to undress. He had just taken off his shirt when he saw Maisie come toward him. She wore a short nightdress and he saw nice firm legs and upturned breasts that pushed tiny points in the garment. Her blue eyes took a moment to move over the muscled beauty of his torso. "You come to visit, talk, or look?" he asked evenly.

She pulled her eyes from his body. "Came to ask questions. What were you talking to Marcy about?"

41

"There a law against that?" Fargo queried.

"I like to know what's going on, especially with Marcy," Maisie said.

"Just what I wanted to find out," Fargo said.

"Did you?"

"Some. Not everything, I'm thinking," he admitted.

"Of course not," Maisie said.

"But she heard me out," Fargo said.

"You ask me anything you want to know about Marcy," Maisie said.

"That's not the way it works, honey. I'll ask you what I want to know about you. I'll ask Marcy about Marcy," he said, keeping his tone pleasant.

The intense blue eyes narrowed a fraction. "You're a challenge," she said.

"You're a puzzle," he answered. She let the hint of a smile touch her lips and walked away, her trim figure controlled, rear hardly moving beneath the short nightdress, each step deliberate. He watched her go into the tent and he finished undressing and lay down on the bedroll and wondered if Marcy would go into the tent. He hoped she would. It might indicate she was responding to his strong words. But she again bedded down on her blanket outside the tent. So much for strong words, he thought.

He let the night grow still before he closed his eyes and let sleep steal over him. The night sounds were tiny, subconscious intrusions as he slept the sleep of the wild creatures, a sleep never total, where the subconscious was always awake. Just beneath the surface of the senses, a kind of instinctive alarm system operated out of its own hidden sensitivities. The half-moon had passed the midnight sky when suddenly he snapped

42

awake, the sense of alarm jabbing into him. He sat up on one elbow and his eyes immediately moved to Marcy. But she wasn't there. Only the empty blanket yawned back at him.

Something was wrong. The overwhelming certainty of it grew out of the same inner sense that had snapped him awake. It had happened to him often enough to dispel conscious doubts. He'd never been able to explain or understand how or why, but every wild creature could attest to the existence of messages that came in their own time and in their own way. He drew on trousers as he rolled to his feet, strapped on his gun belt as he raced for the blanket, his eyes instantly going to the marks on the ground alongside it.

One set of footprints, he saw at once—big footprints, heavy, a man's prints, uneven, the right one digging deeper into the ground. She had been carried over one shoulder, maybe gagged, more likely knocked out. The prints were clear enough in the half-moon, and he followed them down past the edge of the shadbush in a ground-eating, long-legged lope. When the prints suddenly vanished he had to go back for a moment until he found where they had turned into the brush. They continued on through the shadbush, and as he continued on through the foliage he heard the man's voice. He slowed, crept closer, and saw the figure through the foliage, standing over Marcy.

"You've come around. Good. I like a girl awake when I screw her," Eddie Ray said, and Fargo stepped closer on silent footsteps to see the man's heavy lips were parted in anticipation.

"Bastard," Marcy hissed, pain in her voice. Fargo saw

that Eddie Ray had her by the hair as he pulled her head back.

"One thing more, girlie. When I'm finished, you're not telling anybody or I'll kill you, understand? The boys won't give a damn, and if Maisie gives me any trouble I'll kill her," Eddie Ray threatened. He suddenly yanked hard and flung Marcy onto her back. She cried out in pain. Moving with surprising quickness, he swung his body over her, letting go of her hair to pull at the nightdress. Fargo saw a flash of full-fleshed thighs as he rushed forward. Marcy tried to twist away but Eddie Ray had her pinned. He was pushing her legs apart when Fargo's fist smashed into the back of his neck. Eddie Ray gasped in a grunt of pain as he fell away from Marcy. Fargo stepped over her and caught Eddie with a short left hook. The man flew sideways and landed on the ground only inches from Marcy. Eddie Ray yanked at his gun and the Colt flew into Fargo's hand, his finger instantly resting on the trigger.

"Go on, shoot, but girlie gets it," the man said, and Fargo saw the six-gun pointed at Marcy's side.

"Shoot her and you're dead," Fargo said.

"Shoot me and she's dead," the man countered, craftiness in his face, and Fargo swore silently. Eddie Ray was all too right. His finger was on the trigger of the six-gun. A bullet could kill him, but it would also make his finger tighten on the trigger in an automatic physical reaction. Marcy would pay the price for the reflexes of nerves and muscles. Again Fargo swore silently at the man's cunning. "Put the gun down or she's dead either way," Eddie Ray said. Fargo's mouth was a thin, tight line. He had to buy time, a chance for Eddie Ray to make a mistake, a moment, a brief flash of opportunity, a split second. He slowly lowered the Colt to the ground. "Kick it away," the man said, and Fargo pushed the gun with his foot.

"Now turn around, your back to me," Eddie Ray ordered and Fargo obeyed, his every muscle tensed. The man did not want the noise of a shot, Fargo realized. He'd get to that later, when he could muffle the sound. Fargo stayed tensed as he listened to the slight scuffling sound, Eddie Ray's steps coming up behind him. He felt the man close, felt the air move as Eddie Ray lifted his arm to strike downward with the gun. Then something else, another sudden sound, Marcy rolling.

He felt Eddie Ray whirl, reacting to the movement. It was that moment, perhaps the only one he'd have, and Fargo spun, lashing out with his arm as he did. He felt his elbow smash into Eddie Ray's face. "Goddamn," the man cursed as he stumbled sideways, tried to turn, but Fargo's momentum carried him around and he was at Eddie Ray, one hand closing around the man's wrist. He twisted and the gun fell from Eddie Ray's hand. Fargo brought his other fist around in a short uppercut that his foe managed to partly duck, but the blow was powerful enough to send Eddie Ray stumbling backward. Fargo came in with a left hook, but the man was quick and twisted away enough to again avoid the full force of the blow. This time Eddie Ray dived forward, a low lunge that took Fargo by surprise as arms closed around his knees and he felt himself being flung backward. He hit the ground on his back and Eddie Ray closed both hands around Fargo's windpipe. Fargo saw the man's face contorted in fury as he dug fingers into his foe's larynx.

He had the strength of the desperate and Fargo felt the power in his grip. Digging into the ground with both heels, Fargo flung himself upward and Eddie Ray's feet left the ground. His grip loosened at once and Fargo half rolled, enough for the man's left hand to come away from his throat. Using the strength of his powerful thigh muscles, Fargo lifted again as he rolled and Eddie Ray fell away. Swinging to his feet, Fargo saw the man come up to charge again with another diving lunge. Fargo tried to dig his right foot into the ground to get a base for a left hook, but Eddie Ray was already diving. Fargo twisted himself to one side and the diving form hurtled past him.

Eddie Ray landed on the ground on one knee, spun, but this time Fargo's left hook smashed into his jaw and the man hit the ground. He tried to get up as a whistling right came around to mash into his thick lips. Eddie Ray's mouth opened in a cascade of blood and he fell, rolled, then pushed to his feet, swaying with arms held low. Fargo's crashing left and following right seemed to take his head off. He spun in a complete circle before collapsing in a heap where he lay with little streams of red running from his mouth, nose, and one eyebrow. Fargo straightened up, glanced at Marcy. She rested on one knee, her hand on the Colt. She rose as he went to her, handed the revolver to him, and pressed herself against him. He felt the warm softness of her breasts against his naked torso. He held her as she gave a quick shudder and gazed at him, the smoldering eyes suddenly very clear and direct and the pout almost gone from her full lips. She reached up and her lips pressed his, very soft, lingering until she pulled back. "I don't have to say it," she murmured.

"You just did," he said, and a tiny smile touched the full lips just as a low groan came from Eddie Ray. Fargo turned to the man and closed one hand around the back of his shirt collar. "Let's take this piece of garbage back before we get rid of him," Fargo said as he lifted Eddie Ray to his feet. He half pushed, half flung the man forward, watched him stumble and fall and pick himself up and go on at Fargo's next shove. Marcy fell in step beside Fargo as they walked the long way back to the campsite. When they reached the tent, Fargo pushed Eddie Ray to the ground again and saw the fear in the man's battered face. "Get out here," Fargo shouted as he stood over Eddie Ray.

Maisie was the first to appear, stepping from the tent with a robe around herself. Ken Kinnet came into view from behind the tent, the other two men at his heels. Fargo held his Colt pointed at Eddie Ray, who lay half-turned on the ground. Marcy spoke up, tossing words at Maisie. "He was going to rape me. He dragged me from the camp," she said.

Fargo cut in, the gun still aimed at Eddie Ray. "I wanted you to see for yourself before I blow his damn head off," he said.

"Hold on," Ken Kinnet said. "You're not blowing his head off." The man stepped forward and the other two followed, hands half-raised toward their holsters, the threat in their stance. Fargo shifted the Colt.

"Anytime, gents. I'll make it a special—three for the price of one," Fargo said almost softly. The trio halted, sudden uncertainty in their faces as they eyed the big man who confronted them with such cool confidence. Their hands twitched and the seconds passed as they were plainly unwilling to challenge Fargo. Yet they were dangerous, Fargo knew, capable of a stupid mistake to save face.

"There are three of us," Ken Kinnet muttered, with more hope than confidence in his voice.

"I can count," Fargo said.

It was Maisie's voice that cut in, angry sharpness in it. "Stop it, everybody. There'll be no shooting. You're all too important to me."

Ken Kinnet was plainly happy for the interruption and he gestured to Marcy. "She was askin' for it," he said. "We all saw her sashayin' herself around Eddie. She wanted him," Ken Kinnet said.

"That's a damn lie," Marcy cut in.

"It's no matter," Fargo said. "He's done. The only question is how many of you want to go with him." He swept the other three with steel-blue eyes and saw more truculence than confidence in their uneasy stares. But Maisie's voice interrupted again.

"No, there'll be no killing. I need Ken, Tommy, and Josh, and I need you, Fargo," she said.

Fargo frowned at her and nodded his head to where Eddie Ray still lay on the ground. "You can't keep that stinkin' piece of shit around," he growled.

"I won't stay," Marcy said. "I'll run. I won't stay."

Maisie's lips tightened. "That would be awkward, I'll admit," she said, turning to Ken Kinnet. "Come morning, I'll pay him off in full and he rides out of here. The rest of you stay on. No one else gets paid until we're finished. I know you all ride together, but that seems fair to me."

She waited, and Fargo saw the other two men return Ken Kinnet's quick glance. All three were happy to seize on a way out. "I guess maybe that's fair enough," Ken Kinnet said, shrugging with a last show of bravado. "Nobody wants a shoot-out."

"I don't mind," Fargo said.

"That's enough," Maisie snapped. "It's all settled." Two of the others moved and lifted Eddie Ray to his feet. As they walked away with him, Maisie turned to Fargo. "It's the best of a bad bargain," she said.

"It's the worst of a bad bargain," Fargo said.

"I want Ken and the others alive and with me when we find the house. I know what I'm doing," Maisie said.

"Not this time," Fargo grunted.

"Aren't you getting tired of being wrong about me?" she asked.

"Maybe soon," he conceded, and Maisie strode into the tent with the hint of a smile on her lips. Fargo started for his bedroll and found Marcy beside him.

"I'll come stay with you soon as Maisie's asleep. I don't want to be around here till he leaves come morning," she said.

"I'm moving deeper into the shadbush, straight north," he said.

"I'll find you," she said.

"Suit yourself," he nodded, and she hurried back to her blanket while he picked up his bedroll and strode into the thickness of the brush. He halted when he came to a small half-circle where a bed of broom moss offered a soft cushion. He lay down, stripped to his shorts, and put the holster beside the bedroll. He was about to drop off to sleep when he heard her moving through the bushes and he sat up. "Over here," he called, and in moments she appeared, hurrying toward him. She slid down on the bedroll beside him and her dark eyes, quietly smoldering in their liquid depths, moved across his muscled form.

She raised her arms, a slow, deliberate motion, and lifted the nightdress over her head to drop it beside her. He felt his sharp intake of breath at the beauty of her body. She exuded a lush ripeness, all seamless curves flowing smoothly into each other, her body an unbroken tan, plainly the result of nude sunbathing. Deep, full breasts were languid mounds, each tipped by a dark pink nipple on a circle of lighter pink. A full rib cage gave her a rounded torso, and below a short waist was the exciting convexity of a round little belly followed by a luxuriously bushy, unruly dark nap. Her legs moved against each other with smooth-thighed sensuousness. They were youthfully unmarked and firm with very round knees and full-fleshed calves.

Marcy turned to face him and the deep, very round breasts swayed in unison, radiating their own simmering provocativeness. "You sure you want to be this grateful?" he asked.

"Grateful's only a small part of it," Marcy said. "I think we're all on borrowed time. I want to make the most of mine. I want to enjoy before it's too late to enjoy." Fargo shrugged. Her reasoning was as good as any he'd ever heard, and his mouth opened as her lips came to him and he felt the wonderful softness of her breasts against his chest. A small tremor hung on her lips for a moment, then vanished as he probed with his tongue. She gave a murmur and lay back with her arms around his neck and he went with her, feeling the rounded softness of her body, all its seamless contours pressing against him. He found one luscious breast with his lips, drew on it, and Marcy gave a tiny yelp of delight. "Jeez . . . oh, Jeez, yes . . . oh, yes," she whispered.

He drew the sweet mound deeper into his mouth, caressed the deep pink tip with his tongue, and Marcy's full, smooth body lifted, half-turned, slid against his with a rubbing motion. Her legs moved up and down, smooth pressings, sensuous touchings, her round little belly turned to slide back and forth against his groin. Small murmured words came from her. "Good . . . so good . . . more . . . more . . . harder . . . yes, yes . . . good." His hands moved down the soft roundness of her, the seamless, smooth skin that had become hot under his touch, and she was all slow writhing, her entire body an exercise in pleasure. His face buried in the deep, soft breasts, his hands explored, caressed, enjoyed, found the deep, dark unruly nap and pushed through it to feel the venus mound underneath. He felt his own excitement spiraling with hers.

Marcy trembled and a tiny cry escaped her as she felt his throbbing firmness suddenly against her, pressing into the bushy nap, hot against the rise of her pubic mound. "Ohmigod . . . oh, yes . . . yes . . . aaaaah," Marcy said and quivered as his hand moved downward, cupped around the point of the bushy vee, and felt the dampness of her. He touched deeper and found the liquid softness, carnal nectar, that pulled at him at once. Marcy moaned softly as he caressed gently, opening and exploring the soft portal. The moans grew stronger as excitement seized her, until she was gasping out little cries of wanton delight. "Ah, ah, yes . . . oh, please, more, oh, yes," Marcy breathed, and the deep, round breasts rubbed back and forth across his chest as she half twisted in total tactile pleasure.

He felt her full-thighed legs open, then close to press against him, and he moved, swung over her, and slid forward. Marcy's scream was muffled against his chest as his pulsing erectness pushed into her waiting warmth, sliding slowly, sending newly wondrous sensations through her. Marcy began to slide her hips forward and back, immediately falling into her own rhythm of pleasure. Her tiny gasps of breath accompanied each motion. He throbbed against her glabrous walls, taking his own absolute pleasure from her enjoyment, her slow surgings that cried out their own passionate rapture. Slowly, as she continued to writhe and surge with him, he felt the mounting tension grip her and slowness gave way to long spasms, each more intense than the one before it. Marcy's little moans became harsher, and suddenly he felt the sweet contractions of her become inner quiverings. Carried along with her, his own throbbing grew stronger, began to spiral, and as he heard her sudden scream, he felt himself swept away into that glorious instant where all earthly surroundings gave way to absolute pleasure.

"Oh . . . oh . . . ooooooh, dear God . . . aaaaiiiiii," Marcy screamed against him as she clung, arms, legs, torso, everything held against him, round, full breasts pressed into his face as though she could make two bodies one. He heard his own groan of overwhelming pleasure as he stayed with her, encompassed and encompassing, master and slave, possessor and possessed. Finally, Marcy's sigh filled the night, a groan of mixed despair and contentment, and he felt her relax in his arms. "Don't leave," she murmured and he nodded, equally enjoying the embers of passion, tiny throbbings still clinging. He stayed with her until she finally stretched her legs downward and he lay against her and felt her hand rubbing the back of his neck.

"There was just one other time and it was nothing," she murmured. "I was very young. I knew it had to be better. I was right." She settled herself against him and he saw her eyes close and in moments she was alseep, suddenly more girl than woman. He let himself sleep, wrapped in his own contentment. Marcy surprised him by waking just before dawn. He watched her slip the nightgown on and enjoyed the sensuous ripeness of her. "I want to be back before Maisie wakes," she said.

"You that afraid of Maisie?" Fargo asked.

"Guess so. You don't know her. No one crosses Maisie. She's always controlled things, more so since Pa was killed. I can't get my money, and I'm stuck until she finds the damn will or I can get away," Marcy said, and her eyes took on a tiny glimmer. "Maybe you'll change your mind now," she said.

"About what?"

"About staying on here," she slid at him.

"No, but I might hurry finishing that bargain," he said.

"Do that," she said with a satisfied little sniff as she hurried away. Fargo settled back, let himself doze a little longer, and when dawn moved across the sky he rose, used his canteen to wash, and returned to the campsite. Marcy was off to one side, watching as Maisie paid Eddie Ray with a roll of bills. Ray took the money and paused at Ken Kinnet for muttered words before he climbed onto his horse. He cast a glowering look at Fargo from his battered face.

"I'll be seeing you again," he growled.

"That's something you ought to avoid," Fargo said casually, and Eddie Ray rode away at a fast trot. Fargo walked to his own horse. He had just finished saddling the Ovaro when Maisie halted beside him, her high tight breasts pushing little points into the yellow shirt. Her blue eyes searched his face with piercing intentness.

"Marcy come visit you last night?" she asked.

"What makes you think that?" Fargo said as he tightened the cinch.

"I know her. She's different this morning," Maisie said, and Fargo saw suspicion in the gemstone-blue eyes.

"Different how?" he inquired blandly.

"She's bitchy as usual but in a smug way," Maisie said.

"She almost had a bad experience last night." Fargo shrugged.

"She's acting like she's had a very good experience," Maisie snapped, her eyes intent on him.

"You concerned or envious, honey?" Fargo asked mildly.

"Go to hell," Maisie muttered.

"Does that mean our bargain is over?" Fargo asked mildly.

"No, and you know better. It means I decide what goes on around here," Maisie returned.

"Not for me, and you know better," Fargo said and met her narrowed glance with casual unconcern. She spun and strode away. Fargo waited till the tents were down and the others ready to ride. Astride the Ovaro, he drew up before Maisie and the others. "Keep moving north. Don't expect to see me till tonight, maybe not till tomorrow," he said.

"I don't like you disappearing all the time," Maisie said.

"I'm searching," Fargo said.

"Then search with me along," Maisie snapped.

"When we reach Sioux country. I figure that'll be another two days," Fargo said. "Meanwhile, I'm going to try to fix your mistakes." He put the Ovaro into a fast trot and gave her no time to ask more as he rode west through the tall buffalo grass. He circled back soon, after the others had gone north, his eyes scanning the ground until he found Eddie Ray's tracks. He rode at an easy pace, certain where the man's trail would lead him.

4

Eddie Ray rode south, but he made wide sweeps to the east and the west, Fargo saw as he followed the man's trail. Fargo rode patiently, pausing each time Eddie Ray did to note where his quarry often halted to search the mostly flat terrain and then go off again in another direction. Fargo's own plans took shape as he rode. He'd made his decision to take the extra trouble to avoid more killing if he could. There had been too much, all of it the result of highly charged emotions. Now there were others bent on more killing and more revenge. He didn't want to add to the escalation, not until he knew more. The extra trouble might be worth it to everyone, he told himself as he followed Eddie Ray's tracks.

The day slowly stretched into the afternoon and Eddie Ray continued to ride back and forth across the land, which slowly changed into low hills. The first haze of dusk had begun to touch the horizon when Fargo pulled to a halt and peered at the tracks. He saw the hind hoofprints suddenly dig deep into the earth. The horse had been spurred into a sudden gallop. Eddie Ray had caught sight of what he'd been crisscrossing the land to find. Fargo veered the Ovaro to the left and followed the hoofprints. He rode over a low rise and reined to a halt when he saw the distant knot of figures in the last light of the day. He also saw a line of bur oak to his right, steered the horse into the trees, and rode forward another two hundred yards.

Staying inside the bur oak, he dismounted, left the Ovaro, and went forward on foot another twenty yards until he was close enough to clearly see the men as they gathered around a small fire built of a few logs. Fargo smiled as he saw Eddie Ray in the firelight as the dusk turned into dark. The man had done exactly as he had expected him to do. He had come searching for Brad Kelly's brothers. He had no doubt already negotiated his price for leading them to Maisie Wilson. Fargo's eyes scanned the others around the small fire. It wasn't hard to pick out Brad Kelly's brothers. They had the same jutting jaws, the same prominent noses. The other three men were obviously hired help. Fargo stayed on one knee and watched as the men prepared to settle down for the night.

Eddie Ray stretched out some fifteen yards from the others, and Fargo leaned back against one of the oaks. He'd wait for the hour just before dawn, he had decided, when he'd have the dark for what he had to do first and the light for what he planned after. He closed his eyes and let himself doze as the moon made its way across the night sky until he finally woke and rose to his feet. He returned to the Ovaro, took the lariat from the saddle strap, and using the knife from his ankle sheath, cut fourteen lengths of rope. Pushing them into his belt, he slung the rest of the lariat over one shoulder and stepped from the trees. Moving with the silence of a cougar's prowl, he approached the six men nearest each other. Using the butt of his Colt, he brought the gun down on the head of the first figure. The relaxed figure relaxed even more, growing completely limp, and Fargo went to the next man, then the third, and on further until he finished with all six.

He peered across to where Eddie Ray slept and decided to leave him for last. The last of the night was fading away too quickly and Fargo returned to the first of the Kelly brothers. Working with deliberate haste, he tied the man's hands behind his back, then bound his ankles together. When he finished, he went on to the next figure, another of the Kelly brothers, and did the same, pausing to throw a glance at Eddie Ray's sleeping figure before going on to the next man. The new dawn had begun to streak the sky when he finished tying up the last figure, and Fargo had straightened up in the gray light when he heard the sound. He whirled to see Eddie Ray sitting up. *Damn,* he swore under his breath as he saw Eddie Ray frowning, peering across the few yards at him.

The man's frown turned to surprise as he focused on the figure striding toward him, and his hand went to his holster. "Don't try it," Fargo rasped, the Colt leaping into his hand. But Eddie Ray half rolled, half dived sideways and came up shooting. Fargo flung himself flat to avoid the hail of wild yet no less deadly bullets that hurtled all around him. He fired from on his stomach, two shots, and Eddie Ray's body jerked as he started to rise, jerked again, and fell sideways to lie still. Fargo rose and his lips pulled back as he stared down at the lifeless figure. "You were overdue," he muttered and turned away as he heard the groan behind him. One of the Kelly brothers had come around, he saw. Another did the same a moment later, followed by the other bound figures.

Fargo grunted in satisfaction. His timing had been almost perfect. He waited as the six men stared up at him for a long moment. Almost as one, they tried to leap to their feet and bring their hands around but succeeded only in falling and rolling onto their sides. "Goddamn," one swore.

"What in hell," another said.

Fargo watched them in silence until they stopped twisting and rolling to glare up at him, their breath coming hard. One of the Kelly brothers swung himself around enough to sit up. "What is this? Who the hell are you?" he blurted angrily.

"Name's Fargo," the Trailsman said.

The man frowned. "Fargo. You're the one Sheriff Ludlow said ran off with Maisie Wilson."

"Bulls-eye. And you're one of the Kelly brothers," Fargo said.

"Ed Kelly," the man growled. "What the hell do you think you're goin' to do?"

"Give you boys some time to yourselves," Fargo said.

"You're askin' for real trouble," Ed Kelly said.

One of his brothers spoke up. "Untie us now, goddammit, and we'll let you ride out of here alive," he said.

"Look over there at your new friend Eddie Ray," Fargo said and waited as the men glanced at the still form. "You could have ended up like him, but I didn't want that," Fargo said.

"We supposed to say thanks?" one of the brothers bit out.

"Mightn't be a bad idea," Fargo said.

"Why are you helpin' that little bitch?" Ed Kelly asked.

"I'm curious about the truth," Fargo said.

"She killed Brad. You were with her, dammit," the third brother roared.

"She says Brad killed her pa."

"It was self-defense," Ed Kelly said.

"Not according to Maisie Wilson. She says he did it to keep her pa from finding the will."

"Brad wasn't the killing kind. He'd never draw on anyone. Bob Wilson had to draw first," the man insisted angrily.

"Well, now, I don't know that and I won't till we find Davis Kendrick's will. That's why I'm letting you boys stay alive, leastwise till I find that will and see whose name is on it," Fargo said.

"She still killed Brad," the man said.

"Maybe he deserved it," Fargo returned.

"Never," the brother snapped.

"You boys wouldn't be a mite one-sided, would you?" Fargo put out and received a collective glower. He stepped to where Ed Kelly lay and rolled the man against his two brothers, then took the lariat and proceeded to bind them together.

"Jesus, ain't it enough you got us hog-tied hand and foot?" Kelly asked.

"No. This way you won't be able to untie each other. You'll be together longer," Fargo said, and when he finished he did the same with the other three men. Finally he stepped back and surveyed his work. They were all tightly bound together in two groups. He estimated it would take them at least six hours to work loose of the outer ropes and another three to get off the wrist and ankle bonds. He strode to their horses, tied the reins together, and climbed onto the Ovaro.

"What're you doin' with our horses?" one of the brothers shouted.

"You won't be needing them," Fargo said.

"You son of a bitch," one of the Kelly brothers snarled.

"I figure by the time you get untied, walk to a town, find new horses, and start searching again, I'll be real far away. You just relax, enjoy yourselves, and be grateful," Fargo said as he led the horses away. He heard the men shouting curses at him until he was well over the first low hill. The more they cursed and struggled futilely, the longer it'd take them to free themselves. He led the line of horses at a steady pace.

It had gone well, except for Eddie Ray, and Fargo was satisfied as he rode across the flat prairie until he reached another row of low hills and he saw the sun begin to near the horizon. He halted, dismounted, and unsaddled the horses and removed their reins. He shouted and watched the animals run away with new-found freedom. They'd graze, find their own way, perhaps mingle with the herds of wild horses. Fargo climbed back into the saddle and turned northwest. He quickened his pace as the grass grew shorter, anxious to pick up the trail again. Haste makes waste, he knew, yet he allowed himself the twin sins of haste and carelessness. A curse fell from his lips as he suddenly saw the rider coming toward him.

He slowed, his eyes on the figure, which was naked except for a breechclout and a wristband. He glanced to the left, almost certain of what he'd find, and his lips became a thin line. It was not always rewarding to be right, he thought. The second rider wore a breechclout and an anklet and carried a six-foot spear. Fargo gauged distance and dug his heels into his horse, confident there was still time and room for the Ovaro to outrun the short-legged Indian ponies. The powerful black-and-white horse charged forward and the two riders swerved to give chase. But the Ovaro's initial burst of speed had already prevented his being trapped between the two Indians. Fargo bent low in the saddle. He was racing straight forward when, as if by magic, a line of near-naked riders appeared out of the grass in front of him, cutting off his path.

But it had been no magic, he realized. It had been a carefully planned maneuver. Fargo slowed as he yanked the Ovaro around and knew he'd lost at least ten seconds. He sent the Ovaro streaking west, but the first two Indians had closed in from the side. Two arrows streaked over his head, and again he swerved and lost more time. He started east and saw two more riders appear. The line of red men was closing quickly. Fargo swore as he saw that he was boxed in, with not enough room to race past any of his pursuers. Again cursing his carelessness, he hoped to avoid being riddled by arrows and drew to a halt.

The Indians rode up, circling him, and he took in the markings on their wristbands and armbands. Santee Sioux, he noted. One buck, very slender, seemed plainly in command as the others deferred to him as he rode up to face their prisoner. Fargo frowned in surprise as he guessed the youth to be not more than sixteen years old. Arrogance in his face and demeanor, the young buck imperiously held out one hand. Fargo lifted the Colt from its holster and handed it to him. He saw the young buck's eyes widen in surprise as Fargo spoke. "I ride alone," Fargo said in Siouan. He had long ago learned the language, as it was spoken by the preponderance of the plains tribes, including the Crow and the Assiniboin.

The young buck turned a sneering half smile on him. "We do not turn away from one deer," he said, and Fargo winced inwardly. His excuse had been abruptly rejected, but he kept his face impassive. He had but one avenue open to him. He had to stay alive and buy time. At a motion from the very young buck, the others moved forward. Fargo found himself in the center of the band as they moved ahead. They rode east with him across the flat land and onto the long prairie of buffalo grass. They went on until they reached a long, shallow dip in the land.

Fargo's eyes went across the shallow expanse of prairie and saw the brown mass that was a distant herd of buffalo. The Sioux turned left and Fargo saw the camp come into sight. There were six tipis, each with the tripod poles favored by the Santee. He saw skin-stretching racks and drying poles and open pits for fires. A dozen naked children and a sprinkling of bare-breasted squaws were part of the camp. The arrogant, youthful buck took Fargo into the camp and motioned for him to dismount as the rest of the camp hurried to gather around him with a mixture of hostile and curious stares. Fargo, his face impassive, saw one of the tipis open. The flap was pulled back and a tall figure emerged, wearing a bear claw around his neck and deerskin leggings. Fargo saw a severe, lined face with black hair touched by gray. The golden eagle feather of a chief rose from his hair.

Fargo watched the young buck hand his Colt to the chief, who examined the gun with obvious pleasure. The young buck pointed to the Ovaro and the rifle in the saddle case, and the chief nodded. Suddenly Fargo understood the deference paid to the youth. "A good prize, my son," the chief said. Fargo grunted as the older man's eyes hardened on him, stayed on him as he spoke to his son. "He is yours. Enjoy yourselves," the chief said.

"I didn't come to do harm," Fargo said.

"You came to our land. That is enough," the chief said, and Fargo kept his face impassive. There was no room for bargaining, he saw. There was only hate—the hate of the Santee Sioux. Only one thought reverberated inside Fargo. He had to stop them from killing him quickly. He had to buy time at the expense of pain. The double-edged throwing knife was still in his ankle holster. He had to buy time to use it. He had to defer death by inviting it. He had to invoke a more brutal death by enraging them. It would be an exercise in grim perversity, yet it was his only chance.

He half spun as he flung words. "The Sioux are like old women, full of talk," he said, and lashing out with a right hook, slammed his fist into the point of the chief's chin. The chief went down as the shouts of rage erupted, and Fargo felt the others descend on him. He fell, using his arms to cover up as blows were rained on him, but the savage kicks smashed into his back and ribs. He was yanked to his feet to see the chief standing, a trickle of blood running from one corner of his mouth and fury in his face. He raised one hand and pointed imperiously at the prisoner in front of him.

"The special death for him," he said, and the youth cursed in agreement and smashed Fargo across the face with his hand. He turned to the others and spoke words that escaped Fargo's knowledge of Siouan. But he understood the blow that smashed into his back as he was dragged away to the edge of the camp where, in the last light of the day, he was tied to a serviceberry, leather thongs binding him to the tree trunk, his arms at his sides. Though he kept his face expressionless and his back throbbed, he felt a glimmer of satisfaction. He had bought the time he wanted. He'd have the night to try and work himself free. But the moment of hope was short-lived as he saw them put two guards to watch him.

Two stone-faced young bucks, they were not the kind to fall asleep, Fargo knew, and he cursed silently. The chief's son stopped by before the camp prepared for sleep, spit in his face, and spoke to the two guards before striding away. Fargo stayed with his head hanging, watching from half-lowered eyes, and saw the camp settle into sleep for the night. The two guards occasionally spoke to each other but seldom took their eyes from their prisoner. They were some ten feet from him. Fargo silently let the powerful muscles of his arms and back bulge and contract and bulge again in an effort to loosen the thongs without being seen doing so. But he cursed inwardly as with each pause to rest he realized the leather thongs were not loosening.

He stopped, finally, his muscles strained and aching, and let himself doze as the night moved on. He still had hope for his perverse scheme. The Sioux planned no ordinary death for him, and time might yet be on his side. The dawn had just streaked the sky when he snapped awake to the sound of voices. He raised his head to see eight Sioux approaching him. Some carried digging sticks fashioned of elk bone, others carried large, shovel-like implements carved from the shoulder blade of a buffalo, and a few carried long-handled shovels they'd taken from some unfortunate settlers. Fargo was untied and marched to where the son of the chief sat on his pony. While two of the Sioux held him, another wrapped a length of leather around his neck, tightened a knot in it, and he was pulled along as the Indians rode their ponies.

He was taken from the camp, pulled across the short prairie bromegrass as the morning sun began to flood the land. The huge herd of buffalo still idled in the distance, he noted. They finally halted and the chief's son barked orders to the others. Fargo found three of the Sioux holding onto him, while the others began to dig with their assortment of implements. Those wielding the shovels were the most efficient, and as Fargo watched, he saw they were digging a hole. But it was not in the shape of the usual burial grave. This hole was being dug straight downward, he saw, and he felt the curse gathering inside his throat.

He knew the special death they had chosen for him. He had seen the results of it on other Sioux victims, a death of lingering cruelty and terrible pain. Yet it allowed that slender thread of hope he needed to exist. A little time was still left him, if he could find a way to use it. Suddenly, hands seized him and he was being pushed forward, breaking off his thoughts. The Sioux had stopped digging and the hole gaped up at him, a narrow, vertical pit almost six feet deep and just wide enough for him to fit inside. Four of the Sioux held his arms to his sides as they lowered him into the pit, while others instantly began to throw dirt back into the hole. He was held in place until he was packed into the pit with only his head left aboveground.

Fargo's eyes went to the chief's son, who looked down at him with a grin of cruel satisfaction. "This is only the beginning," the Sioux spit at him, wheeled his pony, and rode away. The others followed him. Fargo watched them cross the prairie until they were out of sight. They weren't about to wait around under the burning sun. That ordeal had been left for him. But they'd return to gloat over their torture, he knew. That much was certain. He felt the sun already burning down on him. He had seen others left as he had been left. The relentless rays of the sun baked them, literally cooked their brains. They were first consumed by a terrible, throbbing pain that finally rendered some men broiled into unconsciousness and left others mad. Some lasted for days, finally dying with the skin peeling from their faces, their heads blistered and charred and blackened.

But he had asked for their anger, their special cruelty, he reminded himself, and his reasons still held. They had shoveled the earth back around him, but it was an imperfect seal. Inside the pit he could feel it give as he moved his head in a half-circle. Curling his fingers around his Levi's, he pulled on the fabric and felt the earth move around it. Slowly, he drew one edge of his right trouser leg upward until his fingers touched the ankle holster and then the hilt of the double-edged knife. He drew the blade free of the holster and halted to relieve cramped finger and wrist muscles. As he did, he felt the perspiration running down his face and knew the simple act had taken far longer than he'd hoped it would.

The earth pressing his arm into his side, he used his hand and wrist to thrust sideways with the knife, plunging the blade into the earth that surrounded him. He knew there was no way he could shovel out the earth. Nor could he displace it. But he could loosen it, and once he had enough of it loosened he'd have a chance to move and finally push his way out of the pit. He began to dig, able to use only short, chopping motions that each time loosened precious little dirt. He had to pause every few minutes to give his wrist and fingers a chance to rest.

But he returned to the task each time, swearing softly as he thrust upward, sideways, and downward with the knife, loosening inches of earth each time. He felt the perspiration no longer coating his head and cursed at the meaning of it. He was beyond perspiring. He was being dried out under the relentless rays and knew he had to pause more often to rest. But as he kept on with what seemed an insurmountable task, the spiral of hope stayed with him. He was making progress, painfully slow as it was. The dirt continued to loosen as he thrust and stabbed with the knife. But he was aware of the terrible race that was taking place. He was growing more and more light-headed as the searing sun took its toll, the bouts of dizziness growing more frequent. Yet he could move his arm and let the surge of accomplishment sweep through him.

He could move the knife with longer strokes as he dug deeper into the wall of earth. He dared to cast a split-second glance upward and saw the orange sphere that seemed to blot out the sky still hanging high. Closing his eyes, he renewed his digging, jabbing into the still dense areas of earth, finding new strengths out of desperation. Fighting away the bouts of dizziness that swept over him, he kept jabbing, thrusting, chopping, and when the sun began to slide toward the horizon, he had loosened enough of his vertical coffin so that he could move both his arms and legs.

He halted and felt every muscle of his body trembling. His head felt as though it were about to explode. Resting, his every breath a hoarse rattle, he saw that the sun had begun to slide toward the horizon. He half turned his body inside the confines of the narrow, vertical pit and felt the loosened earth move. His parched, dry throat was the only thing that prevented his shout of joy as he felt the movement around his torso. But he wasn't free yet. Enough of the still hard packed earth remained around his waist and legs to hold him in place. He estimated he'd need another hour of work to be able to push free of his vertical tomb. Though the sun's rays were not as direct, his head began to pound from the cumulative effects of the long day's searing punishment. Fighting back with sheer determination, he ignored the pounding of his head as he swung the knife again inside the pit.

Attacking the sections of earth not yet loosened, he thrust and dug with the blade and felt the pounding of his head grow worse. Almost completely dehydrated, he somehow found the strength to keep digging. The hour was nearing an end when he was suddenly aware of another kind of pounding. He halted the under-the-surface digging to squint across the plains as the dozen riders came into view. They drew to a halt in front of him. Fargo let his head roll to one side as he looked up at the young buck. With a harsh laugh, the chief's son barked commands at the others as Fargo watched from beneath swollen, sunburned eyelids. Unable to catch the Sioux's words, he understood the red man's triumphant sneer. With a wave of his arm, the Sioux led the others away in a gallop as Fargo watched, straining his eyes.

The Sioux were galloping toward the brown mass that stretched across the plains, and when they neared the huge herd of buffalo, separated to come in on both sides of the animals. Fargo's lips worked soundlessly as he cursed with realization. They were going to stampede the buffalo. They were going to drive the stampeding herd over him. Baking him in the pit had only been part of the chief's "special death." This was to be the finish of it. They had left him to suffer the agony of being baked into near unconsciousness, and now they'd add a final gory twist. The stampeding herd would stomp his head into unrecognizable particles. The only thing left might be a stain of blood—and even that might be trampled into the ground beyond recognition.

The Sioux had reached the herd, and using high-pitched screams and racing ponies, they had the buffalo in full stampede in moments. The prairie dust cloud rose at once, partly swallowing up the Sioux, but Fargo knew they were turning the buffalo toward him. Drawing on every bit of strength left in him, he twisted and turned his body, first left, then right, frantic motions as he clawed at the earth with the knife and his hands. He felt the loosened earth giving way as he moved, giving him room to lift his shoulders and lift his arms. He had pulled his arms halfway free when he stopped.

The ground was shaking and he saw the buffalo stampeding at him, only a few dozen yards away, moving with astonishing speed. Their massive heads down, small eyes wide with fear and fury, they pounded toward him, a huge, rolling mass of brown. He'd never have time to pull himself from the pit, he realized. There was no time to escape and there was no place to run, and as the earth shook, he could only stare at the onrushing mass of hooves, horns, and fur.

5

A dozen huge bulls, heads lowered, pounded directly at him, and Fargo could feel the heat of their bodies. With a hoarse cry, he kicked his legs and felt the loose earth move for him. Twisting his shoulders, he took a deep breath and pulled his head into the pit, sinking down as far as he could. The earth shook and pieces of dirt fell on him as the herd stampeded over him and he both felt and heard the thundering sound. The earth continued to shake as the huge herd raced over him, thousands of pounding hooves that sounded like a rumble from hell. Fargo stayed in his earthbound half crouch, his eyes tightly shut as the loose earth rained down on him. The earthshaking pounding seemed to go on forever, but the ground finally ceased its trembling and the awesome sound faded away. Fargo drove his legs deep into the bottom of the pit as he pushed himself upward, forcing his head through the loose dirt.

He'd neared the opening, now covered with new clods of trampled grass, when he heard the sound of hoofbeats coming to a halt directly above him. One horse, he decided, and then he heard the softer thud of footsteps as the rider dropped to the ground. Using his last ounce of strength, Fargo burst from the pit, gulping in air as his arm reached out and up. His hand closed around an ankle and pulled, and he saw the slender figure go down. Fargo was atop the Sioux at once, the knife in his hand, pressed against the throat of the chief's son. Lying half over the youth, Fargo pressed the blade harder against the young buck's throat. "I'll cut off your head," he hissed as he heard the other hoofbeats come to a halt. "You move, they move, you're dead," Fargo said, and saw the fear in the youth's eyes as he knew his life hung by a terribly thin thread.

Fargo used his legs to push himself further out of the pit, pushing the youth with him while the blade stayed against his throat. A quick glance showed Fargo the other Sioux were in a half-circle on their ponies, looking on with uncertainty. "My gun and my horse. Tell them," Fargo said. "Gun, horse, or the son of the chief is dead." The youth, not moving, called out to the others, and after a moment, Fargo saw all but two ride away. The two stayed back a dozen yards and Fargo climbed entirely from the pit, pushed the youth onto his back, and kept the knife against his throat. He fought away a wave of dizziness that passed through him, a reminder that he had precious little strength left in his exhausted, sun-baked body.

He waited and wondered how long he could hold out. Only the lowering dusk told him that time was not standing still. When the sound of hoofbeats reached his ears he didn't move. Not until the horses drew to a halt did he flick a glance upward to see the chief had returned with the others. The chief held his Ovaro, Fargo saw, keeping the knife against the youth's throat. Fargo saw the chief take the Colt and place the gun onto the saddle, and he rose, pulling the youth with him. Holding the knife against the back of the youth's neck, he walked close behind him to the Ovaro, where he took the Colt and exchanged it for the knife as he pressed the gun barrel into the youth's temple. "Let him go," the chief said. "You can ride away."

"Lie across the horse," Fargo said to the man's son. "Facedown."

"I said let him go," the chief repeated.

"Over the horse," Fargo ordered the youth and kept the gun barrel against the boy as he pulled himself onto the Ovaro and lay draped facedown on the horse. Fargo kept the gun on the youth as he pulled himself into the saddle.

"You have my word," the chief said as Fargo slowly turned the horse, the Colt still against the boy's head. "You do not trust the word of a Sioux chief," the Indian said, his voice rising.

"I trust myself," Fargo said as he sent the Ovaro forward at a walk. He cast a glance back at the Sioux. "Come after me and he is dead," Fargo said. The half-circle of Sioux did not move and Fargo saw the chief's eyes boring into him. "That is my word," he added and sent the Ovaro forward.

He kept the horse at a walk as he crossed the prairie in the last light of the day. He rode northward, his head hurting with each step the horse took, and he felt the burning of his face and the exhausted weakness of his body pulling at him, daring him to pass out. But he refused, going on out of some subconscious reservoir of determination. The cool of the night came to help keep him from collapsing. He kept the gun pressed against the youth's head as the moon rose and the prairie terrain changed into low hills and he saw a forest of hackberry rise. He had ridden a good distance, the moon told him as it hung high in the sky, and he halted before the forest and drew the Colt back. "Get off," he said, and the youth slid from the horse's withers. "Tell your father his word is the only reason you live," Fargo said, and he watched the youth quickly stride away to disappear into the night.

Holstering the Colt, Fargo moved the Ovaro forward again as another surge of weakness swept through him. Fighting to stay conscious, he kept the horse at a walk as he rode into the forest. He was threading his way through the trees when he caught the sound of a stream. Nosing the Ovaro to the right, he followed the sound and found a shallow but wide stream that coursed its way through the forest. Sliding from the saddle, he pulled off his clothes and immersed his nakedness in the stream. He pressed his face into the water, turning first to one side and then the other, letting the cool wetness wash over his head as he heard himself murmuring sounds of gratitude.

Finally, he turned on his back, staying in the flowing water of the stream, letting the coolness heal the burning of his head and the aching of his body. The moon rose higher and he stayed in the stream, pulling himself up only when he saw the pale sphere journeying downward across the sky. He rolled out of the water and lay atop a bed of nut moss. The sleep of exhaustion came quickly, and when he finally woke, it was to the sound of morning larks and the cool of the leaves that formed a bower over his head. He immersed himself again in the stream, used a towel from his saddlebag to dry himself, and dressed. He climbed onto the Ovaro and turned the horse north, riding in the shade as often as he could until he finally picked up the trail he sought. The day was nearing an end when he caught up to them, camped between a stand of box elder and serviceberry.

Maisie was the first to stride toward him as he dismounted. "Where the hell have you been?" she demanded, blue eyes blazing.

"The Kelly brothers were on your tail. They won't be now," Fargo said.

"That all?"

"No. I ran into some Santee Sioux."

She searched his face. "You look like you've had trouble."

"I'll be all right after another night's rest," he said and glanced at the site. "This is as good a place as any," he added, and she turned away as he led the Ovaro to one side and began to unsaddle the horse. Marcy appeared before him when he finished.

"I was worried about you," she said.

"Thanks," Fargo said.

"I'll come visit later," she said.

"Only if you want to sleep," he said.

"Two can sleep as cheaply as one," Marcy answered and hurried away. Fargo joined the others for a meal of beans and beef jerky, and when the fire was put out he saw Ken Kinnet with Whitman and Farkas approach him.

"You went after Eddie, didn't you?" Ken Kinnet said.

"He hooked up with the Kelly brothers. I knew he would," Fargo said.

Tommy Farkas leaned forward. "You kill him?" he asked.

"He made it happen," Fargo said.

"He was our friend," Ken Kinnet growled.

"Pick better friends," Fargo said.

74

"When this is over we've some settling to do," Kinnet said.

Fargo half shrugged. "Maybe you'll get smart by then," he returned as they walked away. He took his bedroll and went into the box elder where he undressed to his shorts and stretched out on the bedroll. Exhaustion still held him in its grip and he was about to fall asleep when he heard the soft sound of brush being pushed aside. He sat up and peered through the trees, expecting to see Marcy's soft, full figure. The surprise pushed at him when he saw Maisie step into view, a shirt and a half-slip covering her trim figure.

"Change in plans. Marcy won't be visiting," she said.

"You arrange that?" Fargo asked.

"Yes. I saw her leaving the camp. I knew she was coming to visit you. I told her to forget about it," Maisie said.

"And she just went along with you?" Fargo asked with some surprise.

"Yes. I reminded her of a few things," Maisie said.

"Such as?"

"That's none of your business," Maisie replied sharply.

Fargo peered at her. "Why do you care?" he asked.

"I don't want you having distractions," she said. "I'm still wondering about the other night."

"You're sounding jealous again," Fargo slid at her.

"I'm not the jealous type," Maisie said.

"Bullshit, honey. All women are the jealous type," Fargo snorted. "Marcy's a lot of woman."

Her eyes narrowed at once. "You sound like you know."

He swore inwardly. He'd let himself be too clever. "I'm a good judge of fillies, every kind," he said.

Maisie's eyes softened as she accepted the answer. But only slightly. "She's a child in a woman's body. You'd want more than that," she said.

"Of course," Fargo said and watched her stride away, pause, and glance back at him.

"Now who's full of bullshit," she said and hurried away. He lay down on the bedroll and reminded himself again how dangerous it was to underestimate Maisie.

He slept the night through, and when morning came, Maisie rode beside him as he stayed north and crossed the White River east of the Black Hills. The day grew hot, and it wasn't until he found a good piece of shade in a forest of bitternut that he called a halt. They spread out as they rested in the trees, and he found Marcy beside him.

"Maisie came calling last night," he said.

"Figured she would," Marcy commented.

"She calls the shots," Fargo said, and Marcy shrugged agreement. "What'd she remind you of?" he questioned.

"That she controls everything till I get the money due me. She's right," Marcy said, bitterness in her voice.

"You knew that last time," Fargo reminded her.

"She didn't know. I can't go head-to-head with her. Never could, certainly not now," Marcy said. "You've no right to ask different."

"I'm not," Fargo said.

"You're keeping a promise. I'm keeping reality," Marcy explained.

"I understand. I'll wait. We'll see what time brings," Fargo said.

"It'll bring trouble. Maisie brings trouble," Marcy said and turned away. Fargo's lips pursed and he wondered if

Marcy would prove to be prophetic or just a victim of her own jealousy. When he moved forward again, Maisie rode with him. He drew to a halt when they crossed a low ridge. His eyes narrowed at the edge of a line of plains cottonwoods on a distant rise where he saw the edge of a row of leaves slowly moving in a straight path.

"What is it?" Maisie asked.

"Riders moving through those cottonwoods," he said.

"Indians?"

"You can count on it," he said. He glanced back at Marcy, the three men, and the packhorses. "Goddamn parade," he muttered. "They couldn't miss us. You stay here with them."

"I'm not having you disappear again. I'm going with you," Maisie said.

"You'll all disappear permanently if I don't ride alone," Fargo said, and Maisie's lips tightened. But she stayed as he sent the Ovaro forward. He stayed inside the bitternut forest until he reached the rise and the line of cottonwoods. Moving carefully, he entered the trees, his eyes scanning the ground as he walked the horse forward. He saw the unshod hoofprints, too many lines of them, crossing and recrossing each other. He also saw the slain and skinned carcasses of two elk at different spots in the forest. This territory was full of red men, he thought to himself, and finally drew to a halt when he came in sight of the line of riders as they moved out of the cottonwoods. Ten, he counted, most wearing little but breechclouts. But enough were wearing armbands, gauntlets, and moccasins for him to identify the tribe. They turned west as they rode across open ground. Fargo retreated until he rejoined the others as twilight began to slide across the land.

"Yanktonai Sioux," he said. "They're all over the place."

"Those the ones you got away from yesterday?" Maisie questioned.

"Same cat, different stripes," Fargo said grimly. His eyes went to the sky. "It'll be dark in a half hour. We keep going at a walk, single file." He led the way forward as Maisie dropped behind him. Once again he stayed in the tree cover. When darkness fell he made his way to the edge of the trees to make use of the unobstructed moonlight. But he kept moving forward through the night, over low rises and across open flatland and back to low, rolling terrain again.

"When are we going to stop?" he heard Marcy ask, tiredness in her voice.

"When it's time," he said and led the way up a shallow slope. The moon was on its way toward the horizon when he finally called a halt inside a forest of hackberry that grew thick and deep. "We bed down here," he said.

"I'm exhausted," Marcy said as she slid from her horse, her full, deep breasts bouncing as her feet hit the ground.

"No fires. Cold rations only," Fargo said. "Unsaddle the horses and tether them, same for the packhorses."

"Unsaddling the packhorses will take an hour. We're tired and hungry," Ken Kinnet complained.

"I don't want the sound of pots and pans. Do it," Fargo said and led the Ovaro deeper into the hackberry. When the horses had all been unloaded, the cold meal finished, he returned to the others.

"It's damn near sunup," Kinnet grumbled.

"I know," Fargo said. "You'll sleep through the day. From now on we sleep by day and ride by night. That's the only way we'll get through without being spotted."

"For how long?" Maisie asked.

"Depends. Another few days, I'd guess," Fargo said. He turned and left the others preparing to bed down. Undressed, he stretched out in his own bedroll deep inside the hackberry. He slept quickly, yet stirred soon after when the sun shifted its warmth through the thickness of the foliage. He returned to sleep, and when he woke again the day was drawing toward an end. He used his canteen to wash. Once dressed, he made his way back to the others, who were in various stages of waking. He waited for night to fall before he had the horses saddled. After another cold meal, he led the way out of the hackberry. Keeping the horses at a walk, he continued north, glancing back at the others to be sure everyone stayed in line. It was a ghostly procession under the moon, he observed. The night stayed warm. He kept up a slow, steady pace that brought on its own weariness.

He halted at a stand of shadbush as the moon disappeared over the horizon. "Same as last night. Cold rations after the horses are unsaddled," he said and saw Marcy sink to the ground in exhaustion. It had been a long night, and she was not alone in feeling its effects. He took his bedroll into the thick tree cover, undressed, and slept soundly until he woke with the dusk. He dressed quickly and had everyone moving from the shadbush as the moon rose. Once again, he set a steady pace that covered ground despite its slowness, and by the night's end he was pleased at how much distance they had covered.

"I'm getting used to this," Marcy told him as she paused beside him. "Another night and I might be able to come visiting."

"What happened to being careful?" Fargo questioned.

"It's putting an awful strain on being anxious," Marcy

said, pressing her hand against his groin for a moment before she hurried away. He had them bed down just inside the edge of a small ravine grown over with peachleaf willow. He slept quickly, and the sun still edged its way toward the horizon when he woke. He washed and dressed and led the Ovaro to where the others had bedded down. He was surprised to see Marcy up and dressed, a white shirt tight around her deep, round breasts. "Woke up early," she said at the question in his eyes. "You, too, it seems. Going to try for a start with the day still here?"

"No," he said. "Too risky."

"Good, because you have to wait for Maisie," Marcy said.

He frowned at her. "Wait for her to wake up?" he asked.

"No, wait for her to get back," Marcy said, and Fargo felt the anger and alarm spiral through him at once. "She woke early, too, saw the flash of sun on a lake, and went to take a bath."

"Where, goddammit?" Fargo bit out.

"Over there, past the first rise," Marcy said, pointing, and Fargo caught the sparkle of water in the last of the sun's rays. The lake nestled on the top of a hill, hidden by rocks and bur oak, visible only because of the sun's glint. Ken Kinnet woke and sat up as Fargo cast a quick glance around the spot they'd bedded down.

"She took her horse," he said to Marcy, who nodded. "How long ago?" he asked.

"Ten . . . fifteen minutes," Marcy said.

"Stupid damn girl," Fargo rasped as he dropped the Ovaro's reins over a branch. "Everybody stays here," he said and began to run from the trees, instantly falling into a long, loping gait as he climbed the rise. The sun still hung on the horizon, he saw, its rays too low to any longer glint on the water. He moved upward, crossed small hillside gullies, and the bur oak and rocks grew thicker. His eyes swept the terrain as he moved on silent feet. He was clambering over rocks when the sun disappeared over the horizon. But the lake was before him in the new twilight, an oblong shape with rocks almost entirely around it—a small lake, where clustered growths of penstemons added their pink-lavender hue amid the rocks.

Maisie's clothes were on the shore and he saw her nearby in the lake, turning on her stomach and diving under the surface. He caught a glimpse of a small, glistening rear before she disappeared for a moment, to surface again a dozen feet away. The purple haze in the air told him it was only another fifteen minutes or so before dark as he began to climb down between the rocks. He was nearing the edge of the small lake when he heard Maisie's sharp gasp. He paused in his descent to glance up. His curse was a silent oath as he saw the figure at the water's edge, facing Maisie, who had sunk down to her chin in the lake.

The Indian wore only a breechclout and a pouch hanging against one thigh. His back was beautifully muscled, his body long and lean. Fargo started to pull the Colt out when he paused and let the gun drop back into its holster. If there were others nearby, the sound of a shot would certainly bring them on the run. The Indian took a half-dozen steps into the water toward Maisie, who stared at him, her blue eyes as intense as always but now tinged with fear. Fargo leaped from the rocks to land on the balls of his feet in the soft sand of the shoreline.

But the landing wasn't soft enough and the Indian spun at once, his eyes narrowing as he saw Fargo. He stepped from the shallow water and Fargo saw the Yanktonai Sioux markings on his pouch. The red man drew a bone, jagged-edged scraping knife from his waistband, and Fargo bent down as he pulled his blade from his ankle holster. He waited as the Sioux came toward him, a young, well-muscled, lithe form, his long black hair glistening with fish oil. The Indian feinted with the scraping knife and Fargo pulled back, only to have to duck away again as the Sioux delivered a second quick feint. Fargo countered with his own feint, a quick step to his left, then his right, and an upward swing of his own blade. But the Indian moved with lithe grace, easily avoiding the blow to bring his own weapon down in an overhand arc.

Instead of pulling away, Fargo stepped in and closed his hand around the Sioux's wrist as the Indian brought the knife down. He tried to thrust upward with his own blade and felt the red man catch his wrist. He felt the strength of the Sioux's lean, muscled body, but Fargo used his own strength and his advantage of height and weight. He swung his body in a circle, then another circle, taking the Indian with him. With still another swing, he released his grip on the man's wrist and flung his foe sideways, pulling his own wrist free at the same instant. The Sioux went sprawling, falling at the edge of the water, and Fargo was at him immediately, slicing with his thin, razor-sharp blade.

He cursed as he had to fling himself to one side as the Sioux showed his muscled agility by leaping away from Fargo's slicing arc to thrust up and forward with his own weapon. As he swung himself around to face his opponent, Fargo's eyes swept the lake and saw that Maisie had left the water and stood on the other side of her big bay. The Sioux's knife thrust demanded his attention and Fargo sucked his torso in as the bone blade missed his abdomen by a half-inch. He danced backward, felt the water on his feet and ankles as the Indian came forward in a half crouch, arms hanging loosely, ready to strike in any direction. Moving to his right, Fargo brought his footing out of the water and onto the shore and the Sioux followed, plainly gauging his moves. He feinted, a head-and-shoulder move this time, then lunged with his knife thrusting upward. Again, Fargo barely avoided the blow and twisted away from a follow-up downward slice.

The Sioux had the quickness of a cat, Fargo thought silently as he tried another sideways arc and saw the blow cut only air as his foe danced away. Then with a suddenness that took him off-guard, the Sioux leaped forward as he sliced back and forth with quick, flat blows. Fargo gave ground, unable to find a spot to thrust through the vicious swings. The Sioux kept up the quick, flat slices of his blade, each delivered with such speed Fargo could only give ground. He was still moving backward, trying to find a moment for a counterthrust, when he felt his heel hit the piece of rock. He heard his curse as he went sprawling and felt himself hit the ground hard as he landed on his back. He had only a blurred glimpse of the Sioux's leg striking out, but he felt the pain of the kick that slammed into his hand and sent the knife sailing from his fingers.

He had time only to fling himself sideways as the Sioux's weapon whistled past his head and dug into the ground. Rolling, Fargo regained his feet as he saw the Indian pull his scraping knife from the ground and come at him again. This time, the Sioux's lips were drawn back in a smile of anticipation. Fargo yanked the Colt from its holster. The Indian came forward faster, all too aware that his foe did not want to shoot. Fargo turned the gun in his hand, gripped the weapon by the barrel as he avoided the Sioux's upward thrust. Fargo tried a swiping blow with the butt of the Colt and had to twist away as the Sioux came in low, thrusting short, quick blows. The Indian advanced with new recklessness, executing little leaps with his every slicing blow. Continuing to retreat, Fargo saw the neat pile of Maisie's clothes and shifted to his left to move behind the clothes, her half-slip and shirt on top of the pile.

He halted, facing the Sioux. "Come . . . kill me," he said in Siouan, taunting with his tone. The Indian obliged, moving forward quickly, the bone knife held out in front of him. Fargo stayed in place, gauged split seconds, and as his foe lunged, he kicked out with one leg, sending Maisie's half-slip sailing into the air. The thin garment struck the Sioux's knife hand, instantly enveloping his wrist and arm. It took him but split seconds to shake the fabric loose, but Fargo had calculated on split seconds. He swung the Colt in a short, flat arc and the Sioux's cheekbone erupted in a spurt of red as he went down on one knee. Instantly, Fargo brought the butt of the Colt down with all his strength and saw the man's forehead split almost in two.

The Sioux pitched forward, a deep, groaning sound his last breath before he lay still. Fargo turned the gun in his hand, holstered it and glanced up in the last light of the dusk to see Maisie walking toward him, staying behind the big bay. He stepped back as she maneuvered the horse between him and her clothes, and while she began to dress he strode to where his throwing knife lay. Retrieving the blade, he returned it to his ankle holster and saw Maisie, dressed, come around to the front of the horse. "You goddamn little fool," he hissed.

"I'm sorry," she said. "The day was almost over. I thought it'd be safe."

"Sorry doesn't cut it with me," Fargo said. "You disobey my orders again and our little bargain's over."

"Aren't you forgetting something?" she returned. "You still need me to clear you with Sheriff Ludlow."

"You get me killed and what the sheriff thinks won't matter a damn," he returned. She made no reply, and he pulled himself onto the big bay as night descended to blanket the land. "Get on. I'll take us back," he said, and Maisie swung into the saddle behind him. She rode in silence as he picked his way through the blackness, the warm softness of her pressing against his rear. A moon rose to help him find his way, and he finally reached the place where he'd left the others. Maisie slid to the ground and Fargo dismounted and strode to the Ovaro.

"You were long," Marcy said. "You have trouble?"

"Some," he allowed laconically, climbing onto his horse. "Had to kill a Sioux." He took in the others with a single, tight-lipped glance. "We move out right away. When that Sioux doesn't return to his friends, they'll come looking for him. I want to be as far away as I can get when they do. You can eat in the saddle while you ride," he said. Maisie made no protest and Ken Kinnet and Tommy Farkas took the packhorses in tow as they started after Fargo. The moon, largely covered by scudding clouds, afforded little light, but Fargo was grateful for that. He took a long circle away from the lake that cost him at least two hours, and he didn't call a halt till near midnight.

Peering through the darkness, he saw that the prairie buffalo grass was growing thinner and the South Dakota rock formations more frequent, rising up in the night. He made out distant pinnacles and towers as well as buttresses and breathed a sigh of satisfaction. This was Dusty Smith's land. And the Sioux's, he reminded himself.

The moon hadn't reached the horizon when they halted inside a cover of thick shadbush, where a long plain stretched out beyond. He took his bedroll under one arm after unsaddling the Ovaro. Maisie moved toward him. "Where are you going?" she asked, and he saw Marcy nearby, listening.

"There's a rise in back of us. I'll be up there. I want a good look at the land from up high when morning comes," he told her.

"We getting close?" she questioned.

"Maybe," he said. "My friend Dusty Smith carved a place for himself near here."

"Good," Maisie said and surprised him with a warm smile before she walked away. He went on up the tree-covered slope, aware of Marcy watching him go. When he found a spot almost at the top of the rise, he stretched out his bedroll. The moon still hung over the horizon line. He undressed, lay on the bedroll, and wondered if this was the night Marcy would find the courage and the moment to come visit. But the reality of what still lay ahead occupied most of his thoughts. Finding Dusty Smith was the first objective. Was he still alive? Fargo wondered, aware that the answer held the key to going on. Finding Davis Kendrick's house, and staying alive, would be a matter of pure luck if Dusty was gone. And Dusty had had a lot of years on him the last time they met, Fargo recalled.

The sound cut into his thoughts, footsteps climbing the rise, brushing aside low weeds. He sat up and saw the figure moving through the trees. "Over here," he called softly and felt the astonishment spinning through him as the figure came closer.

"Hello," Maisie said, stepping to where he sat on the bedroll. "Surprised?"

"Yes," he admitted, but decided against telling her why. "You came to apologize?"

"I wouldn't say that," Maisie replied.

"No, not you," he grunted. "Guilty conscience?"

"Maybe, but I mostly came because I want you to know how I feel," she said. She wore her robe wrapped around her, but he saw a flash of one long, lovely leg as she lowered herself to the bedroll. "We need each other, Fargo. I need you to find that house and the will. You need me to clear your name. But it's more than a bargain. It's a bond," Maisie said, leaning closer. "People that bond should be close," she said, her arms lifting, sliding around his neck, and then her mouth was on his, pressing, her lips surprisingly soft. She pulled back, her hands going to the robe, and a second later the robe lay at the edge of the bedroll and she was beautifully naked in front of him. A tiny smile was on her lips as she watched his eyes move over her.

He took in square shoulders, pronounced collarbones, a skin that was lightly tanned. Her breasts were full enough, turned upward, each tipped by a small areola, lightly pink, with little pink nipples that gave her a girlish look. Her rib cage was pronounced, not an ounce of excess flesh on it, and his eyes went to the flat abdomen and below it, an equally flat belly that moved to a surprisingly dense but small triangle. Her legs were almost thin. Maisie was all of a piece, he concluded, everything taut and firm about her, her body exuding a sensuous intensity that matched the gemstone eyes. She half turned, came against him, and he felt the burning hotness of her at once as her fingers pulled at his drawers, pulling them from him, and he knew he was responding instantly. "Oh, Jesus . . . oh, yes," Maisie whispered, her eyes widening, desire and approval in her gasp. Her hand reached out, closed around him, and she gave another gasped cry at the touch. "Oh, God, oh, God," she murmured, and then his hands were around her back, pulling her down to him.

She came at his pull but her fingers stayed around him, moving with eager gentleness, touching, caressing, stroking, and he was throbbing, fully blossomed for her. She brought her hips upward, pressed the small, dense triangle to him, and rubbed herself up and down against him. He felt himself growing, throbbing eagerly, immersed in the overwhelming grip of the sensual. Maisie gave a gasped cry as his mouth found one upturned breast. His lips closed around the edge of the small areola, sucking against its slightly raised soft little rim. He felt the gossamer, filamentlike hairs that edged the small circle, strangely exciting, and he continued to caress the upturned mound with his tongue and lips. Finally pulling back, he saw the pink tips had grown fuller, firmer, each a tiny surrogate messenger of the flesh.

Maisie's hands moved up and down his body, over his torso, his rump, and pressed into his powerful thighs as he drew first one breast and then the other into his mouth. "Oh, God . . . oh, so good, so good," she murmured, and he let one hand explore, trace a slow trail across her tight, firm abdomen, down across the taut flesh between her hips, and then push through the dense little nap. "Oh, yes, yes, yes . . . go on, go on," she breathed as his hand pressed down on the swelling of her Venus mound. His hand slid further downward as her lean legs moved to open and then come together, but not before he felt the dampness of her inner thighs. Maisie moaned little gasps and her hips pushed upward, the body offering itself with eager desire. "Take me . . . Jesus, take me," she murmured, and Fargo's hand slipped upward, between her thighs and closed around the wet portal.

Overwhelming pleasure swirled through him as he touched her, liquid velvet, passionately arousing, and he touched deeper, caressing the tight velvet walls. "Yes, yes, yes," Maisie breathed and pulled his face back against her breasts. She began to make quick, spasmlike motions with her torso as he touched deeper, caressing the liquescent tunnel. "Yes, yes . . . more, oh, more," she gasped out, a half whisper, half cry, and her hips twisted, lifted, offering all of her secret places to him. He felt her hands clutching at his buttocks, pulling him to her, and he shifted and brought his throbbing rod to the edge of the waiting portal. Maisie screamed in glorious response as he slid forward, deeper, still deeper, and her body began to buck under him, quick upward thrustings as her legs clasped and unclasped and clasped again against him.

No slow surgings for Maisie, every movement an echo of the sharp intensity in her blue eyes. Her ponytail tossed from side to side as her head lifted and fell back again. "Jesus, yes, yes, yes . . . iiiiaaaa. . . ." Maisie screamed, a sharp sound punctuated by shrill little cries as she jammed her crotch into his and he knew the pleasures of his own pulsating ecstasy, that surfeit of the senses that seemed to go beyond bearing and then went further. Maisie's upturned breasts bounced in unison with her every wild spasm, and he saw her blue eyes staring at him, seeing yet unseeing, her lips moving with sharp cries of absolute pleasure. Unsure of his ability to hold back much longer, he cried out as he felt her tightening around him, velvet contractions that quickened with instant intensity, and he heard his own cry of pleasure mingling with Maisie's scream. "Oh, God, yes, yes, yes . . . now, it's now, oh, God . . . ," she managed before words became a long, high scream against his chest and Maisie's entire body bucked and leaped in a wild passion that rejected all control.

But with an angry half cry, Maisie's frenzied spasms grew less, until they were but little twitches of the flesh, inner and outer. Finally she lay still yet clung to him, and the intense eyes searched his face. "I knew it'd be like this with you," she said, relaxing with abruptness, her body going limp except for the firmness of her breasts. "Now, aren't you glad you waited for a real woman instead of an immature girl?"

"Aren't you glad you decided to change from ice to fire?" he countered.

She thought for a moment. "They both have their place. Ice protects. Fire consumes—including itself."

"And you don't like to be consumed," he offered.

"I like to be in charge," Maisie said.

"You sorry?" He smiled.

She leaned against him, breasts soft points into his chest, her taut, lean body wrapped around him. "I'm never sorry for anything," Maisie said. "That was just a sample of what we can have together if you stick with me."

"I liked the sample," he said. "But samples are never satisfying."

A little smile crossed her lips as she raised herself and pushed one upturned mound into his mouth. "I don't want you to be unsatisfied," she said, and he felt her hand reach down to hold him, stroking, smoothing, even as she kept her breast against his lips, giving and getting at the same time, sensuously reveling in the simultaneous exchange. Fargo knew he wasn't going to be unsatisfied.

6

Maisie had been everything she'd been before and more, her frenzied desires turning words into flesh, explanations into ecstasy until finally she lay beside him and slept. He watched her and marveled at how she seemed to exude intensity even when asleep, the taut firmness never leaving her body, the dense, small triangle its own statement, the upturned breasts constantly waiting. He dozed with her until he heard her wake and he snapped his eyes open. She was sitting up, reaching for the robe. "I want to be back before the others wake," she said.

"You care what Ken Kinnet and the others think?" he asked.

"I care what they know, not what they think," she said.

"I still don't understand why you insisted on bringing them along. I told you we wouldn't need them," Fargo said.

"It's not over yet," Maisie said as she began to put on the robe.

"What happens if no one finds the will, if it has just disappeared?" Fargo questioned.

"If there is no will, if it can't be found, all of Davis Kendrick's property will be up for grabs. Anyone can file a claim with the territory claims office for the property and the mine," Maisie said.

"Would you do that?" Fargo asked.

"I might," she said.

"You think the Kelly brothers would?"

"Probably. Of course, nobody can file a claim until it's plain that the will is lost. That's why finding the will is so important, not only to prove Pa is the inheritor but to stop anyone from filing a claim," Maisie said and rose as she wrapped the robe around her. "It'll all work out. You wait and see," she smiled confidently, paused, let her lips linger on his for a moment before hurrying away as the first streaks of dawn touched the sky.

He lay back on the bedroll and dozed another hour, waking to the morning sun. After he dressed, he climbed to the top of the rise and let his eyes sweep the land. The South Dakota rock formations rose high amid the mostly flat terrain, but he was still too far away to see the things he needed to see so he made his way back down to where the others were waking. Maisie, still in her robe, poked her head from the tent set up between the shadbush as Fargo began to saddle the Ovaro.

"You stay here. Everybody stays until I get back," he said.

"Where are you going?" she asked.

"To find a better place for you to stay," he said.

"Thought you didn't want to ride in the daylight," she said.

"I don't want a damn parade riding in the daylight," he corrected sharply, and she disappeared into the tent. He finished saddling the horse and started to lead the animal from the tree cover when Marcy stepped out from behind a tall shadbush. He saw the fury in her round-cheeked face.

"Bastard," Marcy spit out at him.

"What's eating you?" Fargo asked, even as he suddenly feared he knew the answer.

"I saw Maisie go look for you. I expected she'd be back soon. I just didn't believe it, not any of it," Marcy hissed.

"Believe what?" Fargo asked as he swore silently.

"That you'd screw her, that she'd do it. I didn't believe it. God, how could I have been so wrong," Marcy said.

"Aren't you jumping to conclusions?" Fargo returned evenly.

"Did you tell her we did it?" Marcy questioned, dismissing his answering question with disdain.

"No, I didn't tell her that," Fargo said, letting himself sound injured.

"Afraid she wouldn't if you did?" Marcy said waspishly.

"Saw no reason to tell her," Fargo said.

"Maybe I'll tell her. I'd enjoy that," Marcy threw back defiantly.

"Your call," Fargo said, deciding on perhaps the only course that might deflect her hurt fury. "But didn't you say you couldn't afford to antagonize Maisie?" he reminded her.

Marcy's mouth thinned. "You don't care?" she slid at him, a trace of petulance in her voice.

"Makes no mind to me," he lied, maintaining his position.

"Then it makes no mind to me, and you can go to hell, Fargo," Marcy said, and Fargo breathed a silent sigh of relief. He hadn't been happy at the prospect of two furious females, especially Maisie with her icy unpredictability. But his approach had worked; reality pulled on Marcy and he climbed onto the Ovaro as she glared at him, "If you think she's going to level with you because you laid her, you're a fool," Marcy flung at him. "She tell you about Davis Kendrick's warning?" Fargo frowned back and she gave a satisfied snort as she spun on her heel and strode away.

He moved the Ovaro forward out of the shadbush as the furrow stayed on his brow, his eyes sweeping the new morning land. He saw no signs of movement and sent the horse into the open as he made for the first rock formation that rose from the largely flat terrain. It turned out to be a basalt bridge, and after examining it, he moved on. He rode to the other rock formations that rose up from the dry bedrock terrain and halted to explore natural stone bridges, small mesas, massive clay pillars, sandstone buttresses, red clay formations of pedestal rocks, and tall basalt pinnacles. He explored each of the red and gray formations before going on to the next as he also took note of the shallow pony prints in the ground. Dismounting at each, he went over the trails with his fingers. A few were only a day old but none were fresh. But there were many trail marks, too damned many. The Sioux rode this land in large numbers.

It was past midday and the sun was brutally hot when he found a spot that satisfied him—a rock formation known as desert windows. Openings cut through narrow ridges and layered rock called ribs. These desert windows were sandwiched between sandstone buttresses and went back deep into the stone. Best of all, they'd be all but undetectable alongside the towering red-toned buttresses. He uttered a grunt of satisfaction and began to retrace his steps, carefully making mental notes of the various formations as markers. Halfway back to where he'd left the others, he spied the horses and figures moving toward him and he immediately took the Ovaro behind a cluster of tall gray rock pinnacles. He dismounted and climbed into a crevice that let him see the Sioux as they passed some hundred yards away. With surprise, he saw women and children with travois, along with a dozen near-naked braves. They traveled north, which told him there had to be a Sioux mainline camp not that far away.

When the Indians moved from sight, he mounted the Ovaro and continued his own journey. Dusk had begun to settle over the land when he reached the shadbush and saw that Ken Kinnet and Josh Whitman were awake. They watched him dismount. Maisie appeared from the tent minutes later, and then Tommy Farkas joined Kinnet and Whitman. Marcy was the last to appear, and she waited off by herself. Fargo peered at Maisie's face and knew at once that Marcy hadn't told her anything.

"I was getting worried," Maisie said.

"Get ready to ride," he told her.

The night came down as he led the procession from the shadbush and onto the open land. The moon rose to outline the massive rock formations, and Fargo used each as a marker to guide his way. With a rest stop to water the horses at a sinkhole, the night was nearly gone when they reached the sandstone buttresses and the deep desert windows between them. He dismounted and gestured to the four cavelike openings. "The packhorses in one, the rest of you spread yourselves out in the others. You'll be safer here than anywhere else till I get back.

Stay asleep through the day, as usual. There's a fault trough in back with water from an underground stream. You can use it at night, but be sure you don't leave anything out where it'll be seen—a blouse, scarf, hair ribbon, hat, anything."

"You saw Sioux?" Ken Kinnet asked.

"All over the place," Fargo said. "Now I'm going to get me some rest before I start out again." He led the Ovaro into the first of the desert windows, went as deep as the cave would go, and spread out his bedroll. He was asleep in moments. When he woke, the others were out of sight, hidden away in the other cavelike stones, and he grunted in satisfaction. The sun had risen past the midday sky as he saddled the pinto. He'd need daylight for the kind of riding and searching he had to do. He swung onto the horse.

"You'd better come back," the voice said, and he turned in the saddle to see Marcy at the edge of one of the other stone windows.

"You get over being mad?" he asked.

"No. I just don't want to die out here," she said.

"And I want that will," Maisie's voice cut in. He saw her step from inside the opening.

He fastened a small frown on her. "By the way, what's this about Davis Kendrick's warning?" he queried.

Maisie's eyes went to Marcy, blue fire at once. "Can't you ever keep your mouth shut?" she snapped.

Marcy gave a diffident half shrug. "Didn't know I had to. I thought you'd told him everything," she said with studied casualness.

"Suppose you tell me about it," Fargo cut in, and Maisie returned her eyes to him.

"Davis Kendrick told everyone that they were forbidden to go to the house. It was strictly his, for his own use when he got older. He said anyone entering the house would find himself killed," Maisie said. "No exceptions."

"He hid the place, but he wanted to make sure no one got the idea of trying to find it," Marcy said. "I told you, he was a clever madman."

Fargo's frown stayed on Maisie. "Why didn't you mention this to me?" he asked.

"Didn't think it was important—an old man's warning, probably nothing but a hollow threat," Maisie said.

"Anything else you didn't think important?" Fargo questioned.

"No," she said calmly. "You certainly don't believe in an old man's wild threat."

"I don't know, seeing as how you're not sure yourself," Fargo said, and Maisie's eyes narrowed.

"Meaning what?" she asked.

"*Probably* nothing but a hollow threat, you said. *Probably.*"

"Just a word," she said. "But seeing as it's question time, I've been wondering how you expect to find your friend Dusty Smith. How come he stays alive out here in the middle of Sioux country?"

"A long time ago, Dusty came upon an Indian boy with a broken leg. He set it in a splint and took the boy back to his tribe. They showed their thanks by letting him live out here without being bothered," Fargo said. "Anything more?"

"Just be careful," Marcy cut in, and Maisie nodded agreement as he moved the Ovaro forward into the afternoon sun. He rode without glancing backward at them, suddenly wanting to find the damn house and be finished with the strange relationships and involvements in which he found himself. He set a steady pace north, scanning the land as he rode, watching for any sign of riders. By dusk he had crossed the White River into the badlands and found a spot to bed down. He was in the saddle again with the new day, keeping the horse at a steady trot.

He drew on memory as he recalled the three basalt pinnacles that marked the spot where Dusty Smith had his shack, two tall spires with a short one in between. The day neared a close when he reined to a halt atop a caprock mound and felt the excitement pull at him. The set of pinnacles rose up directly ahead and he put the Ovaro into a canter, rounded one side of the rock formation to see the small but sturdy shack behind it, crafted of oak and the same volcanic rock that formed the massive pillars and buttresses that dotted the land. A flood of relief went through him as the door of the shack opened. Fargo dismounted in front of the structure, his eyes on the short, stocky, gray-haired figure that stepped forward. Dusty's square face was held together by an unusually grainy skin that gave him a grayish color and earned him the sobriquet of "Dusty." Fargo saw the sharp blue eyes peer at him from under gray brows that furrowed.

"You don't look a day older, Dusty," Fargo said, and the square face broke into a surprised grin.

"Fargo. By God, it's you," the older man said. "Good God, it's been a helluva long time."

"It has," Fargo agreed as he clasped hands with Dusty Smith.

"Come in, come in," Dusty said, moving toward the house with a shuffling gait. Fargo followed him inside.

The big room seemed exactly as he'd last seen it, a comfortable feel to it with big, open ceiling beams, and in the center of the floor, a worn but comfortable sofa. One wall of the room was still covered with leather and hide pouches, soft canteens, traveling bags, and money belts of all sizes and shapes. His eyes paused to admire one large traveling bag fashioned of a particularly fine elk hide.

"Still making your pouches, I see," he said.

"And still going to Rapid City twice a year with them," Dusty said, setting out a crock of whiskey and two clay cups. "What in tarnation brings you this way, Fargo?" he asked.

"I came to see you, old friend," Fargo said and raised his cup in a salute. The whiskey was good-bodied and smooth, but then Dusty had always abhorred poor whiskey, he remembered. "I'm wondering if you ever heard about a man named Davis Kendrick," Fargo questioned.

Dusty Smith let his lips purse in thought. "Can't say that I have," he answered.

"He was a strange bird. He was supposed to have built a house out here someplace," Fargo said.

Dusty's brows lifted. "Oh, that feller. Yes, he was a strange one from everything I heard," Dusty said. "Heard all kinds of stories about that house."

"I've been hired to find it," Fargo said. "You know where it is?"

"Not exactly, but northeast somewhere. There's a big stand of Douglas fir that grew itself down near Bison. I heard he had the place built in the middle of the forest there," Dusty said.

"I was told he brought a whole crew of Italian

builders to put up the place. You ever see any of them?" Fargo asked.

"No, but that's one of the strange stories that surrounds the place. A prospector found three of those Italians in a streambed, all shot dead. Then an army patrol found another four dead in a dry sinkhole."

"The Sioux get them?" Fargo questioned.

"No. The Sioux won't touch the house. They say it's a bad place. They call it the place of evil spirits," Dusty said.

"Maybe the Sioux know a lot more than we do about evil spirits," Fargo said.

"I won't argue that," Dusty agreed. "There's something else. It seems none of those Italian carpenters ever returned from the job. Some had left wives in Rapid City who tried to find out what happened to their husbands."

"Did they?"

"No. They even got the army to look, but the troops never found anything but the four they'd found in the sinkhole," Dusty said.

"They find Davis Kendrick's house?"

"No. Nobody knew where to look for it."

"You knew," Fargo said. "You just told me."

"They never came asking."

"How do you know?"

"The Sioux came visiting. They bring me hides once in a while. They told me about this strange house of evil spirits. They're afraid of it. It's become a big taboo with them. You know Indians. Good spirits and evil spirits are part of the world."

"Yes. They give offerings to the one and use the shaman's magic against the other."

"I think Davis Kendrick was able to go back and forth

to his house because they saw him as an evil spirit, part of the house, somebody to avoid."

Fargo nodded agreement and finished the whiskey. He wanted to move on, but he also knew Dusty would be offended if he didn't spend more time, so he accepted his old friend's invitation to stay the night. They spent it telling old stories of old times until sleep overtook them both. He left in the morning after a breakfast of buckwheat cakes Dusty made with practice and enthusiasm. He set the Ovaro northwest across the badlands. Again he rode with his eyes sweeping the terrain for signs of Indian ponies. He came onto fresh trails but nothing else. The terrain grew less dry, a coating of downy bromegrass softening the stone underfoot. He saw clusters of bitternut and ironwood as he rode through the afternoon.

The sun had begun its slide toward the horizon line when he spotted the first of the Douglas fir. Excitement catching at him, he put the pinto into a canter and saw more of the big trees with their reddish cones. The sun had begun to dip below the horizon when he came to the wide expanse of firs and nosed the horse into the trees. Their size, perhaps the largest tree next to the giant sequoias, allowed for plenty of space between the straight trunks; and when the moon rose, it afforded more than enough pale light for him to keep moving. He hadn't gone far into the forest of giant trees when he spied the small piece of land that had been cleared. Guiding the horse toward it, he reined to a halt at the edge of the circular area to stare at the house that rose up in the center of the clearing.

He heard the soft sound of his breath being sucked in in a silent exclamation. The house was unlike any he had ever seen, except in pictures. It rose out of a surrounding bed of tall green sagebrush and was more of a dark castle than a house, with twin spires rising on each side and turreted windows in a wide-beamed dark center section. It sat glowering, forbidding, menacing. In the pale moonlight it seemed to shimmer with a malignant evil, as though it had been transplanted from another time in another land—some mountaintop in seventeenth-century Europe, a place of caped figures, spells, and potions. It was little wonder that the Sioux saw it as a place of evil spirits.

Fargo moved through the surrounding sagebrush as he edged the pinto forward. The eerie, shimmering structure did not grow any less malevolent as he drew closer, and he felt himself jump as a flock of bats erupted from the dark eaves with a rush of wings. He swore at his attack of nerves and steadied the pinto as he peered again at the house. The base was of stone but the rest had been crafted of wood, beautifully fashioned despite its forbidding appearance. He saw only a single tall door as he guided the horse around the perimeter of the cleared area, the rest of the house offering only the narrow, turreted windows. He felt the Ovaro pull sideways as he walked the horse around the strange house. Even the horse picked up the eerie aura of the place, he noted grimly. At the other side of the house he saw a square structure, the door hanging open to show the stalls of a stable inside.

It looked even more ordinary than the average stable alongside the brooding, ominous house. Completing his circle of the house, he turned the pinto into the trees and moved through the forest to halt at the very edge, where he spotted a place to bed down. The moon had passed the midnight sky when he drew sleep around himself on his bedroll, glad to clear the foreboding image of the house from his consciousness.

When morning dawned he began to make his way back the way he'd come, avoiding three parties of Sioux and skirting Dusty's place as he again made mental markers to map his route. He spent the night beside a small stream in a clump of cottonwoods and kept a steady pace the next day. The great rock formations dotted the dry land again, and he sought out those he'd used as his guideposts. By the time the day began to draw to an end, he reached the low rise of caprock that lay before the desert windows where he'd left the others. Urging the Ovaro into a trot, he crested the top of the mound, and he reined to a halt as he spied the three near-naked riders racing their ponies past the desert windows. The gunfire came mostly from inside the rock caves as the Indians raced past, but then he saw another two Sioux on foot, crouched at the edge of the buttress, pouring shots into the rock openings.

"Shit," Fargo swore as he drew the big Henry from its saddle holster and put the pinto into a gallop. The thousand yards of land was mostly flat, but the Sioux were concentrating on their quarry inside the caves. The two crouched on foot didn't see him until he was almost upon them. Finally they heard the sound of another horse and turned. Fargo rode with the big Henry to his shoulder and fired two shots. The first Sioux flung his arms into the air as he flew backward, the second one getting off a single shot that went wild as Fargo's shot smashed into his chest.

But the three on horseback had turned and were racing back toward him as Fargo skidded to a halt and leaped from the saddle. Two arrows and a bullet slammed into the ground a foot from where he landed, diving and then rolling to duck behind an edge of the rock formation. He brought the Henry around as he saw two of the bucks race past him, firing a shot that missed as the two riders swerved. As he waited for the third to race by, he heard a faint sound at his back. Whirling, he caught a glimpse of the Sioux diving at him from atop the rock. He managed to brace himself as he raised the rifle defensively with both hands. The Sioux landed hard on him and he went down, onto his back. But the upraised rifle had done its part, catching his attacker in the chest with enough force to deflect the blow from the tomahawk the Sioux tried to bring down. Taking but a second to recover, the Sioux came at him again with the short-handled ax upraised. Fargo saw he had neither the time nor enough space to bring the rifle around to shoot. Cursing, he let the Henry fall from his hands and managed to close his fingers around the Sioux's right wrist and grab the man's throat with his other hand.

He held the Indian off for a moment and glimpsed another Sioux racing toward him on his pony, bowstring drawn back, arrow about to hurtle through the air. Fargo held the Sioux in his grip a split second longer and saw the arrow leave the bow, on its way to plunge into him. Using all his strength, he swung the Sioux sideways. Still holding onto the Indian's wrist, he saw the man's mouth fall open, his eyes grow wide, and felt the impact as the arrow hurtled into the Sioux's back. The Indian fell forward, the tomahawk dropping from his hand. Fargo released his grip and rolled to one side as he yanked at the Colt. The Sioux on horseback had whirled his pony around and started back at him to fire another arrow when the Colt barked. The Indian jerked as though he'd been kicked by his pony before he toppled from his mount.

Fargo swung the Colt in a half-circle as he saw the third Sioux appear. But the Indian yanked his pony around and raced away, vanishing across the flat, hard land before Fargo rose to his feet. He holstered the Colt and retrieved the rifle before stepping out in front of the desert windows. "Anybody hurt in there?" he called. Maisie was the first to emerge.

"Nobody here," she said, and Fargo saw Marcy appear behind her. He turned to the next cavelike opening and saw Ken Kinnet walk out, Farkas and Whitman at his heels.

"Nobody here, either," Kinnet said.

Fargo swept them with an angry glance. "What the hell happened? Let me guess. You went to the water and left something—just what I warned you not to do," he said.

Maisie answered first. "We went before daybreak. It was still dark. We didn't even know something had been left until they suddenly were in front of us."

"They were going to come in at us, searching for us. We had to shoot," Ken Kinnet said.

"What did they find?" Fargo asked grimly.

"It was my hand mirror. I took it with me when I went to the water to wash. It must've fallen out of my pocket when I came back. I don't know how they even saw a little mirror from way in the distance."

"They saw the sun hitting it," Fargo snapped. "You might as well have left a damn lantern," he said and turned to Maisie. "Get the packhorses. One of your visitors got away. You can be sure he'll be back with friends. We've an hour of daylight left. Let's ride the hell out of it," he said.

Marcy paused beside him as she went to get her horse. "I'm sorry," she said, no defensiveness in her tone.

"I warned you about leaving anything out there. You should've been more careful," he said coldly, unwilling to let her feel atonement with an apology. She walked on, her round-cheeked face glum. He swung onto the Ovaro, rode out a few yards to scan the fading light until Maisie and the others rode up, Marcy at the rear, Ken Kinnet and Farkas leading the packhorses. "Ride and ride hard," Fargo rasped and set the Ovaro into a gallop.

He kept up the fast pace until dusk turned to dark and then slowed, but only to a canter alongside a long wall of limestone, finally halting when the moon was high. "We bed down here," he said, swinging to the ground. "Eat quickly and get to sleep. You'll be riding hard again come morning."

"What happened to riding only by night?" Maisie asked.

"That's been screwed up. The Sioux will come back looking for us now, and they won't have any trouble picking up our trail. But they won't trail by night. That'll give us time to rest here. But come morning they'll be trailing us again and now they'll check every rock formation along the way. We'll have to make time. Checking every rock formation will slow them some, but not that much. They'll keep coming, you can be sure of that. They might even pick up some more help along the way."

Maisie settled herself with a strip of cold jerky and cast a little frown his way. "You haven't told me what happened to you," she said. "You find your friend?"

"I found your house," Fargo said, and the jerky fell from Maisie's hands as she leaped to her feet.

"You found the house?" she said, clutching at him. "Oh, God, that's great." Her mouth pressed his for an instant. "That'll keep me riding forever."

"Sioux arrows will keep me riding," Fargo said.

"You saw the house yourself?" Maisie asked excitedly.

"I did. It's not like any house I ever saw before," Fargo said.

"Davis Kendrick was not like most men," Maisie said.

"He was a crazy man," Marcy's voice cut in. "Everybody that worked for him knew it. If he hadn't paid so well, Pa would've left him long ago. I'd bet Brad Kelly would have, too."

"Forget about what Brad Kelly might have done. The only thing that matters now is finding the will," Maisie said, a touch of reprimand in her voice.

"That's the only thing that matters to you," Marcy shot back and walked away, suddenly looking very disconsolate and lost.

Maisie watched her go with disdain. "She takes after Pa. She'll never have any steel in her," Maisie said.

"Bed down. We've hard riding tomorrow," Fargo told her and she walked into the deep shadows against the limestone wall. After he unsaddled the Ovaro, Fargo took his bedroll and made his way in the other direction against the stone wall. Then he spied the blanketed form a few dozen yards from the others. He walked toward it and halted. Marcy's eyes were shut tightly.

"You're not asleep," he said.

She opened her eyes and sat up to glower at him. "I might have been," she said.

"No, you're still stewing," he said. "You think I was too hard on you."

The half pout came to her face. "You could try being understanding. I should've been more careful. I made a mistake, but mistakes happen."

"And out here a mistake can mean you're dead," he said, not unkindly. "Apologies won't help. Being sorry won't help. Not making mistakes is the only thing that counts. I wanted you to keep that burned inside you."

Her glower softened and her nightdress shifted to show the curve of one round, deep breast, making him sorry he was so tired. "You want me to say thank you?" she offered.

"No, I want you to remember that," he said.

"I will," she said. "I'll remember everything about this trip, the good and the bad."

"That'll make two of us," Fargo said. "Now, get to sleep." Marcy lay back on the blanket obediently. He wanted to stay with her. She was as unhappy and disconsolate as when he'd first met her, a time that seemed so much longer ago than it was. But he walked on to the end of the limestone wall, where he set out his bedroll and slept.

7

When he woke with the first gray light of the day, he found Maisie dressed and waking the others, eager anticipation bursting from her. She wore a yellow shirt and tan riding britches that fit her exuberance and her body with equal perfection. "Let's get moving. We can get at least an hour's head start on them," she said.

"Guess again," Fargo grunted. "They'll be riding with the dawn. But that's all the more reason for us to move." He saddled the Ovaro and checked the packhorses, which thankfully were holding up well. Marcy again brought up the rear as Fargo led the way northwest, skirting the front edge of the limestone wall. He kept everyone at a fast canter and slowed only when the sun grew very hot. As the day wore on, he dropped back from time to time to scan the land behind them; but as the day began to near an end, he still hadn't glimpsed any signs of the Sioux.

He wondered if they had gotten lucky, if the Sioux had given up the chase. But he knew it was too much to hope for. It would be out of character. Tenacity was a Sioux trait. It wasn't like them to give up. Yet by the day's end they had seen no pursuers. The terrain was beginning to change. They were drawing closer to the forest of Douglas fir, but the night descended and Fargo called a halt at a stream in a line of red cedar that had taken root much farther west than it ordinarily did. The pace he'd set had fatigued everyone, including the horses. "How much further?" Maisie asked, weariness and impatience in her voice.

"We'll be there tomorrow," he told her, and she brightened at once.

"We'll do a lot of celebrating soon," she half whispered to him. "Promise."

"Sounds good," he said, aware of Marcy's eyes on him as Maisie went off to erect her tent. He stopped beside her as she gathered up her blanket. The lost, disconsolate air still clung to her, he saw, not helped any by exhaustion. "Hang in there. It'll be over soon," he said.

"Meaning we're getting near the house."

"That's right," he said.

"What happens to you then?" Marcy asked.

"Maisie has some things to clear up with Sheriff Ludlow in Redrock. Then I'll be on my way," he said. "That was our bargain."

Marcy gave him a long, thoughtful glance. "She'll probably stick to it," Marcy said slowly. "Maisie always knows when to strike and when to back off, when she can use someone and when she can't. She'll discard some people like old clothes and treat others like jewels. She always knows how, who, and when. You shouldn't ever underestimate Maisie."

"I've learned that," Fargo said. "You're very different than Maisie. Maybe that's why you don't like each other."

"She says I'm soft inside, that I'll never have any steel."

"I know."

"She has contempt for me because of that. But I'm happy the way I am. I wouldn't want to be like her," Marcy said with a kind of pouty pride.

"Go to sleep," he said almost gruffly and walked on as he wondered how two sisters could be so different. But then he'd seen that before. Blood could bind and it could separate, he reflected. He found a spot and undressed, stretched out on his bedroll, and let tiredness sweep him into instant sleep. The new sun woke him in the morning, and after dressing he scanned the terrain over which they had come. Nothing moved and he felt more uneasy than hopeful. Maisie had the others up and ready to ride soon after, and he led the way northwest, again setting a good pace over the land now that the downy bromegrass added comfort to the horses' feet.

It was into the midafternoon when he halted at a sinkhole fed by an underground stream to water the horses and let everyone rest. He stretched out on the ground, let himself relax, and watched the others. Maisie was the only one who refused to relax. She paced back and forth, checked the gear on the packhorses, paced again. They were getting close to the Douglas firs, Fargo knew, but a sixth sense told him the horses needed a good rest and he ignored Maisie's sharp glances. Finally, she stalked over to him. "I thought you were worried about the Sioux catching up to us," she threw at him.

"I am. That's why I want these horses rested when they do," he said, and Maisie angrily strode away. He lay back, closed his eyes for a few minutes more, then suddenly snapped them open. He'd heard nothing and certainly seen nothing. But he had felt the vibrations in the ground and instantly knew their message. Leaping to his feet, Fargo vaulted onto the Ovaro. *"Ride!"* he shouted in Maisie's startled face. Galvanized into action by his urgent cry, the others ran to their horses and scrambled into their saddles to follow Fargo, who already had his pinto at a full gallop. He waited till the others were into a gallop before he turned in the saddle to look back.

Still in the distance, the Sioux came into sight, first one batch, then two more bands a few dozen yards on each side of the first ones in the center. At least thirty in all, he guessed as Maisie brought her big bay alongside him. "Why the three bands?" she asked.

"To head us off if we turn in either direction," Fargo explained.

"Are we turning?" she questioned.

"No. We're riding straight as fast and as far as we can," he said with a glance back at the others. Marcy was in the rear, Ken Kinnet near her, with Farkas and Whitman leading the packhorses. Fargo swore into the wind as he raced the Ovaro toward the trees that rose in the distance, Maisie's big bay doing a good job of staying with him. He led the way over low mounds, past clusters of tall sagebrush, and saw the Douglas firs come into distant view. He didn't have to glance back to know the Sioux were gaining, and he cast a quick glance skyward. The dusk hung in the air, the sun was beginning to near the horizon, and his lips pulled back in a grimace. He could hear the high-pitched shouts of the Sioux now, and the forest he raced to reach still seemed too far away. "The packhorses are slowing us down. We should let them go," he said to Maisie.

"All our rations are on them," she protested.

Fargo shrugged. The group surged forward, drawing every ounce of reserve from their mounts. Marcy still brought up the rear, but she wasn't losing any ground, he noted, spurring the Ovaro forward again. Running a full length ahead of the others, he saw the wide expanse of the Douglas firs rise up in front of him. Looking back, he saw the Sioux closing in fast, the three bands closer to each other. Most had bows, but a few had rifles, Fargo noted, and plunged the pinto into the forest. "Don't slow down," he called to the others. "There's room to ride hard."

"Not hard enough. They'll sure catch us in this forest," Maisie said.

"Not if I'm right," Fargo said, skirting a giant fir as he said a silent prayer and remembered what Dusty Smith had told him about the Sioux and the house. If he was right, it was the only chance to save their scalps. The cleared land suddenly loomed up in front of him and he charged across the sagebrush toward Davis Kendrick's malevolent house. He raced through the sage to the very door of the house, where he reined up and skidded to a halt. The others came to a stop alongside him, and he turned and looked back at the Sioux. They had come to a stop at the edge of the cleared land. Fargo heard the deep breath escape his lips.

He watched the Sioux milling back and forth, chattering amongst themselves, staying at the edge of the cleared land, some moving back into the trees. "What is it? Why aren't they coming after us?" Maisie frowned.

"The house," Fargo said.

"The house?" she echoed.

"They believe it's a place of the evil spirits. They won't come closer," Fargo said.

"How'd you know that?" Ken Kinnet asked.

"Dusty Smith told me. I hoped to hell he wasn't

wrong. He wasn't," Fargo said. He moved a dozen yards away from the house but left plenty of cleared land between himself and the Sioux. The Indians didn't move forward as they watched him return to Maisie and the others.

"Now what?" Maisie questioned.

"They're going to keep their distance, it seems," Fargo said, then wondered if he'd have to take back his words as the Sioux began to move their ponies. But as he watched he saw them make a circle around the perimeter of the cleared land, staying just inside the trees, until they had the house surrounded.

"What are they doing?" Maisie asked.

"They won't come any closer, but they're making sure we don't get away," Fargo said.

"How long will they stay there?" Marcy queried.

"They'll stay until we do something to try and get out," Fargo said. "It's a kind of Mexican standoff."

"Then let them stay there while I search for the will. We've enough rations for another two weeks," Maisie said. "Maybe they'll get tired of their little circle and pull out on their own. If not, we'll find a way to sneak out when we're ready."

"Maybe," Fargo allowed as he dismounted and dropped the Ovaro's reins over a hardy clump of sagebrush, not nearly as confident as Maisie that they could sneak out. But for now, she had a point. She could go ahead and search for the will. He watched her slide from the big bay and stand before the house.

"It is a weird place," she commented.

"It gives me the shivers," Marcy said. "The Sioux are right. There's something evil about it."

"You're being as superstitious as the damn Indians,"

Maisie sneered. "It'll be dark soon," she said, turning to Tommy Farkas. "Go into the place and find the lamps, Tommy. There have to be lamps inside."

Maisie led her horse to a spot where she could tether him on a gnarled length of broken tree trunk. Tommy Farkas strode to the door of the house. Her eyes were on the man, Fargo saw, as Tommy opened the door of the house and went inside. It was but a second later that the explosion shattered the air. Fargo whirled to see Tommy Farkas blown out of the doorway of the house on the unmistakable blast of a shotgun. Tommy Farkas hit the ground on his back, his chest torn open and bubbling scarlet, and lay still. "Christ," Fargo breathed.

He stepped past the man's lifeless body to peer into the house through the open doorway. Just inside a small foyer entrance, the shotgun lay positioned on the floor, the barrel raised to point upward. Scanning the surrounding area, Fargo spied the length of thin trip wire that ran across the floor right behind the doorway. Unseen by Farkas as he stepped into the house, he had hit his leg against the trip wire rigged to the trigger of the shotgun. The booby trap had worked with absolute efficiency. Fargo spotted a second wire, less than a foot behind the first, also running to the trigger of the shotgun, plainly designed to set off a second blast from the weapon.

Fargo stepped back to where the others still stared at Tommy Farkas's lifeless form. Except for Maisie. She had followed Fargo's eyes and now turned to tug at Josh Whitman's sleeve. "Go to the back. See if there's a rear door," she said.

"There isn't," Fargo cut in. "But there's a tall window at the back of the house."

"Go in through the window," Maisie ordered Whitman. "Break it if you have to and disarm that damn shotgun from the rear."

Whitman nodded and quickly started to edge his way around the house, staying close to the outer wall as he cast nervous glances at the Sioux. Fargo watched the Sioux and saw that they didn't move. He followed Whitman to the corner of the house and let the man disappear around the other side. Fargo stepped back to where Maisie waited impatiently, one foot tapping the ground. Fargo listened for the sound of breaking glass but there was none. "He must have gotten the window open," he said to Maisie, and the words had barely left his lips when a second explosion ripped through the dusk. "Goddamn," Fargo swore as he sprinted around the house, casting a glance at the Sioux, who still formed a circle at the edge of the clearing. Once again, they didn't move. Fargo skidded to a halt at the tall window, which had been opened.

He peered inside. Josh Whitman sprawled on the floor, only half his head still with him. Another shotgun had been positioned to face the window. Booby-trapped identically to the one at the front door, its wire ran slightly higher from the floor to trip anyone climbing in through the window. It also had a second wire, lower to the floor and a half a foot back. Clever, efficiently and deadly clever, Fargo grunted and decided to take no chances with other, possibly unseen wires. He drew his revolver and took aim at the trigger of the shotgun where the second wire still ran to set it off. He fired and the shotgun blasted its second barrel as the bullet smashed into the trigger and the wire, its shot going off into the wall as the gun fell from its mount.

It lay harmless on the floor, trigger all but severed, the

wire torn away. Fargo swung over the window and dropped to the floor on the balls of his feet. He stepped past the device and Josh Whitman's body, saw a kerosene lamp in one corner of the room and lighted it as the gloom began to descend quickly in the house. He crossed a large living room furnished with two settees and two stuffed chairs. One wall bore a collection of cattle skulls arranged in a cluster, as though they were huddled together grazing—except for the absence of their bodies. The two curved spires on either side of the house had spiral stairways leading from the center of the house to a second floor.

Fargo also noticed a room with books and a wooden desk as he walked through the living room. He saw two more kerosene lamps, lighted both, and the room flooded with light. Reaching the foyer entranceway, he saw Maisie outside through the open doorway. Her face relaxed as she saw him. He halted behind the shotgun, raised the Colt, fired and destroyed the first booby trap as he had the one at the rear window. Ken Kinnet rushed into the house, Maisie following with more calm, and Marcy appearing last. "Josh?" Ken Kinnet asked him.

"Dead. Same thing," Fargo answered.

"Goddamn bastard," Ken Kinnet cursed the spirit of Davis Kendrick. "Son of a bitch had everything rigged and waiting. Who the hell would've figured that?" Fargo let his eyes find Maisie's. She met his stare and looked away, her face a mask of lovely iciness. "I'm going to bury Tommy and Josh," Ken Kinnet said. "You goin' to help me?"

"Fargo will help you," Maisie said. "Bury them against the wall outside."

Ken Kinnet frowned inquiringly at Fargo, who nodded back. "Pull them outside. I'll be along in a minute," he said and stepped back as Kinnet dragged both bodies out of the house. Fargo's eyes stayed on Maisie, the furrow deepening on his brow as she ignored him and surveyed the room.

"What a weird place," she commented.

"I think I'm beginning to understand something," Fargo slid at her, and she finally turned to stare back at him, the usually piercing eyes covered with a cool, almost innocent veil.

"What would that be?" Maisie asked.

"Why you insisted on bringing them along," Fargo said, his face grim. "You knew about Kendrick's warning. You called it a hollow threat, but you weren't about to test it out yourself. That's what you meant when you said they'd come in handy. Tell me I'm wrong. Christ, tell me that."

The blue eyes remained veiled. "I should resent that, but I'm going to make believe I didn't hear it," Maisie said.

"And make believe he's wrong," Marcy cut in.

Maisie whirled on her. "You shut your bitchy little mouth," she hissed. Fargo continued to stare at Maisie with a kind of awe and realized he desperately didn't want to believe what he was thinking. Ken Kinnet's voice interrupted his thoughts.

"You comin' to help me?" the man shouted, and Fargo wrestled his eyes from Maisie's cool, unflustered stare to stride from the house. Outside, Ken Kinnet was using a small shovel from one of the packhorses and handed Fargo a spade. "This is the best I can do," he said as Fargo took the spade and began to dig alongside him. They dug a shallow grave and Fargo let Ken push his two friends into the pit as darkness descended. The lamplight from the house gave them just enough illumination to shovel the earth back over the hole. When they finished, the moon had climbed into the sky and Ken Kinnet stared across the cleared land to the trees. "They gonna stay there?" he asked.

"Yes," Fargo said. "Let's get the gear inside and unload the packhorses." Ken Kinnet followed as he went outside, unsaddled the Ovaro, and began taking rations and other gear from the packhorses. Maisie appeared and took her saddle pouch and the smaller handbag she carried with her at almost all times. When Fargo went into the house for the last trip, he saw Maisie looking thoughtfully at one of the spiral stairways.

"We'll explore up there in the morning when there's more light," she said. "There's plenty of room for everyone to sleep down here." Fargo turned and saw Marcy at the door, peering into the night.

"What about them? They could sneak up on us while we're asleep," she said.

"Maybe we should take turns standing guard," Kinnet put in.

"You'd have to patrol the whole house. Besides, there's no need. They don't want to come anywhere near the place. Nothing that's happened here tonight is going to make them change their minds about it being a place of evil spirits," Fargo said and threw a glance at Maisie. She refused to meet his eyes and began to unpack her things.

"Marcy and I will sleep in the other room," she said.

"I'll sleep outside," Fargo said.

Maisie's glance was cool and chiding. "You afraid of evil spirits?" she queried.

"The air's cleaner out there," he said and saw the blue eyes narrow at him.

"Suit yourself," Maisie said and turned from him. He took his bedroll outside and set it down in front of the door, his glance going to the line of dark figures that were as if carved there amid the trees, silent and unmoving. Undressing, he lay down on the bedroll, the Colt by his side. He had fallen asleep when a sound woke him, the click of the door latch, and he sat up to see Marcy in her short nightdress.

"Everyone's asleep. I couldn't fall asleep. Thought some of that clean air might help me," she said and knelt down beside him.

"I underestimated Maisie," Fargo said. "I knew she had drive and determination and that she was damn clever at getting what she wanted. I just didn't think she'd be that ruthless."

"Me, neither. Maybe we're being too hard on her. Maybe she didn't think about that when she brought them along," Marcy said.

"Sudden attack of sisterly sympathy?" Fargo asked with surprise.

Marcy shrugged. "I guess so. I told you Maisie says I have no steel inside. Here's more proof."

"Maybe it's only proof that you can't bring yourself to believe some things and that makes you caring, not weak."

"And maybe you're just being kind," Marcy said with a wistful half smile. "But you can't say I didn't warn you." She rose abruptly and started to turn away, then paused. "I hope you're sorry," she half pouted.

"About what? That I underestimated Maisie?"

"That you laid her," Marcy snapped.

"I never said I did," he answered.

"You never said you didn't," Marcy tossed back as she hurried away. He lay back on the bedroll, glad she'd given him no time to find an answer. He pulled sleep around himself and slept until the first rays of the sun woke him. Blinking his eyes open, he peered across the cleared land to the trees and instantly sat up. The Sioux were up on their ponies, and as he watched he saw a new line of riders appear. They moved into the trees and spread out as the other Sioux began to leave. They were changing the guard and the meaning became all too clear: they had no intention of withdrawing.

Fargo rose, his lips tight, drew on trousers and boots and strapped on his gun belt. Carrying his shirt over one arm, he opened the door and strode into the house to find Maisie already dressed and in the center of the room. He saw Marcy in the doorway to the other room, still brushing her hair. "Where's Kinnet?" he frowned.

"He just went upstairs to have a look around," Maisie said. The words still hung on her lips when the scream spiraled down the staircase, Kinnet's voice in a hoarse cry of pain that ended abruptly in a shuddering sound and a dull thud. "My God," Maisie gasped as Fargo began to go up the stairs, two steps at a time. He came to a halt when he found Ken Kinnet at the top of the staircase.

A long, heavy piece of steel, sharpened at one end to make it into a wicked spear, had smashed through Ken Kinnet's skull, all but cutting it in two, coming out at the base of his throat. A length of cord still hung from the other end of the weapon. It ran to a hole in the ceiling. Fargo's eyes went to the side of the top step and saw the wire that ran to the edge of the hole in the ceiling. When

Kinnet's foot had come down on the top step he triggered the wire to the hole in the ceiling and the steel spear had been released. Davis Kendrick had plainly enjoyed devising the deadly traps he had set, and he'd done all too good a job. Fargo turned and went down the spiral stairway to find Maisie and Marcy at the bottom, staring up at him.

"He's dead. Another booby trap," Fargo said.

"Good God," Marcy breathed.

"I'm thinking the whole damn house is booby-trapped," Fargo said, fastening his eyes on Maisie. "You send Kinnet up there?"

Her eyes hardened at once. "I told him to have a look upstairs. I certainly didn't think there'd be another booby trap up there."

"You didn't take any chances though, did you? You didn't go up yourself," Fargo said.

"I came to find the will, not be stupid," Maisie snapped icily.

"And that includes using sacrificial lambs," Fargo said.

"That includes doing whatever I have to do," Maisie said.

"Right now that means one thing for all of us," Fargo said. "Finding every trap Kendrick set if we want to stay alive. That means searching this weird house inch by inch."

"How do we do it without getting ourselves killed?" Marcy asked.

"Very carefully. First you get yourself a long stick. One of those shotguns I disabled will do. Then, you don't take a step anywhere without using the stick to explore your way. You climb a stairway, you press each step with your stick before you step on it. You don't open a door, not even a closet, unless you're standing back and to one side. Then after the door's open, you sweep the walls and the floor with your stick before you go on. You make like you're a blind man, only you stay back further. When you're in a room, you don't open a bureau drawer without using your stick and staying to one side. You got all that?"

"Yes," Maisie said, and Marcy nodded, her face grave.

"It could take the better part of the day. Don't even think of looking for that will until we're finished," Fargo said to Maisie. "If you set off a trap, you yell out so the rest of us will know you're all right," he finished.

"I'll take the right wing upstairs, Marcy will take the left," Maisie said.

"I'll go over the rest of this floor and the cellar," Fargo said and waited as Marcy and Maisie picked up the shotguns. He climbed the stairs and dragged Ken Kinnet down and outside, where he deposited the man's lifeless figure atop the grave he'd helped dig. Fargo's eyes swept the trees and saw the Sioux staying quietly in place around the house. He went to the Ovaro and took his lariat back to the house with him to where Maisie and Marcy waited. "Anybody meets a door that won't open or something you can't search, call me," he said and paused a moment to watch Marcy start to edge her way up one of the spiral stairways. "Slow and careful," he reminded her, and she nodded as she pounded each step with the butt of the shotgun.

Fargo found the kitchen of the house, saw a long-handled splint broom, and took it with him. He began to cautiously explore a room adjoining the living room. It appeared to be a study, with shelves for books yet to come. He had just finished in the room when he heard the heavy crash and then Marcy's voice. "I'm all right," she called. "It was another of those steel rods." Fargo blew a sigh of relief through his tight lips and went on to another room. Its door was closed. He took his lariat in one hand and had started to twirl it in a tight circle when the shot exploded from upstairs in the right wing. Maisie's voice followed instantly. "A damn six-gun hidden in a niche in the wall," she said, sounding more angry than frightened.

He returned to twirling the lariat and flung the rope with a quick wrist motion that saw the loop land around the knob of the door. Standing to one side, he pulled hard and the door came open, followed instantly by a double blast of gunfire. He let a second go by for the gunsmoke to dissipate before he could see the two rifles rigged up together atop a chair and pointed at the door. "I'm all right," he shouted back and used the lariat again, this time to toss the loop over both rifles and yank them to the floor. Stepping into the room, he saw where the wires had been cleverly affixed to the guns to let them fire when the door was pulled open.

He surveyed the rest of the room and saw a bed and a large dresser, along with another chair. Using the handle of the broom, again standing to one side, he managed to pull open the drawers of the dresser, carefully working each one halfway open. They were not trapped. He scanned the rest of the room and found no more devices. Walking back through the living room, he went into the kitchen and saw another closed door. Using the lariat again, he yanked the door open. There was no shotgun blast. But he saw the steps that led down to the cellar, and using his broom handle again, he leaned forward and pounded the first step. He jumped back as the cascade of two-by-fours smashed down from above the lintel, landing on the top step and clattering down the others. Anyone standing on the step would have been killed by the shower of planks. Fargo cursed as he shouted out to the others.

Shoving aside the two-by-fours, he sent them clattering down the rest of the stairs and followed. The cellar was made of thick stone walls and a stone floor, a dim, almost dark, place. He spied a lantern and lighted it. An adjoining area could be seen through an arched stone entranceway, and moving the broom ahead of him to scrape the sides of the arch, he entered the second area. It was smaller than the first, also made of stone, but the floor was sandy soil. As he raised the lantern higher, he saw one corner of the area covered with pale white objects. Stepping closer, the objects became bones—skeletal remains, human bones, skulls, arm and leg bones, pelvises.

He stared down at the scene, dropped to one knee, and set down the lantern. Counting, he came up with fourteen skulls. He scanned the collection of bones again, paying special attention to breastbones and ribs. When he finished, he examined each skull by hand, finally putting down the last as he pushed to his feet. The grim discovery lay silently before him, a chilling testimonial to ruthless madness. Fargo took his lantern and left to go into the larger cellar area. He put down the lantern, turned it out, and climbed the stairs to the floor above. Maisie and Marcy were waiting. Outside, the day had moved into afternoon. The careful, painstaking search for the devices had taken time. He saw Maisie glance out the window.

"I'll start looking for the will after we eat," she said.

"I found the remains of the foreign workmen he brought here to build his damn house," Fargo said. "Those the army didn't find."

"The remains?" Marcy echoed, her eyes widening.

"Their bones are in the cellar. They were murdered," Fargo said.

"My God," Marcy breathed.

"They were poisoned somehow, I'd guess maybe in their food," Fargo said.

"What makes you think that?" Maisie asked.

"No bullet holes in any of the bones," Fargo said. "Davis Kendrick made sure no one went home to tell about his house. He was a goddamn madman. You were right, Marcy."

"Madman or not, he left a will, and I'm going to find it. That's all I care about," Maisie said.

"I know," Fargo grunted and heard the bitterness in his voice as Maisie went to her traveling bag and took two strips of jerky out, handed Marcy one, and sat down in a chair with the other.

"Don't dawdle. I want to get started searching, and you're going to help me," she said to Marcy. Fargo saw Marcy meet his glance with a shrug.

"I've nothing better to do," Marcy said. "And the sooner she finds the damn will, the sooner we can get out of here."

"Aren't you forgetting something?" Fargo said and nodded outside to where the Sioux waited.

"You said they might get tired and quit," Marcy reminded him.

"I said maybe," Fargo answered and walked outside to the Ovaro, where he took a beef strip from his saddlebag

126

and slowly ate as his eyes swept the figures in the trees. They had spread out to surround the house more evenly, he noted, standing with unmoving patience until others would come to relieve them. He swore under his breath. When he finished eating, dusk had begun to gather. He went inside, where Maisie had two lanterns lighted. She walked to one of the adjoining rooms.

"We'll start in here," she said to Marcy. "Look into every corner, underneath every table, in every nook and cranny, behind every drape, and under every rug. I'll take all the bureaus and tables. God knows where that lunatic has hidden it." She paused to glance at Fargo. "You could help," she said.

"This is your party," he said.

"You can't just bow out," Maisie said.

"I'm not bowing out. I've kept my part of the bargain. I found the damn house for you. The rest is up to you, and I don't want to be part of it," Fargo said.

"You're disappointed in me. That's your problem," Maisie said. "But I know you'll concentrate on getting us out of here. You want to make sure I keep my part of the bargain."

"Bulls-eye, honey," Fargo said and walked from the house as the dusk deepened. Outside, he dug a shallow grave beside the one where the other two men lay and pushed Ken Kinnet into it. Night had descended by the time he finished, and as the moon rose he saw the Sioux stirring. Soon after, another band appeared and changed places with others, who rode away. The new set took their places surrounding the house. Fargo went inside as Maisie came down the spiral stairs, Marcy behind her.

"We're stopping for the night. I don't want to search in the dark, even with a lantern. We might miss something," Maisie said. "You figure a way to get us out of here?"

"Not yet," Fargo said. "Right now, I'm wondering if our best chance is to sit tight and outwait them. They watched us bury three of us. They'll see that as more proof that this is a place of evil spirits."

"I'm thinking they're right," Marcy said. "This is a place of murder, death, and madness. If that's not evil spirits, I don't know what is."

"It'll do," Fargo agreed.

"I've no patience with superstitious rot. I'm going to turn in," Maisie said and strode into the next room, taking the small handbag she kept with her.

"Me, too," Marcy said to Fargo. "Searching all day for those damn booby traps took a lot out of me." Fargo nodded and as Marcy passed him he saw the fear and the strain in her face. She was the only innocent victim in all that was falling around her ears. He had made a bargain with Maisie, Ken Kinnet and the others had hired on for money, the Kelly brothers had a stake in finding the will. But Marcy had been dragged along, trapped—maybe weak, but a victim nonetheless. He felt sorry for her as he watched her disappear into the other room.

He pulled off his shirt, lay down, and waited for the night to bring sleep to him. It almost did.

8

The drums woke him. He had begun to drift into sleep when he sat up and took a moment to bring the sound into focus. Pulling on his shirt and gun belt, he went to the door of the darkened room and peered out into the night. The drums didn't come from the Sioux at the edge of the trees. They were distant, at least a mile away, he guessed, yet carrying clearly through the night. He heard Maisie and Marcy behind him and motioned for them to be silent. They obeyed, until Maisie finally whispered to him.

"What are they doing?" she asked.

"I don't know," he said. "But drums always have a meaning." He continued to listen and his lips drew back in distaste as he took in the steady beat, the sound familiar yet unfamiliar. "I don't like it," he murmured. "It sounds like war drums, but different."

"Maybe they're beating drums to keep away evil spirits," Marcy suggested.

"That's possible, but then maybe they're working themselves up to something," Fargo said. "I think I better find out."

"How?" Maisie asked.

"By taking a look for myself. That means sneaking

through their lines," he said. "I think I can do it, alone." He moved back into the house. "You two go back to sleep. I want them to think everyone in here is asleep. I don't want them alert."

"I'll be quiet. I'm not sure I can sleep," Marcy said.

"That'll do," Fargo said and started toward the door.

"I don't like this. It's too risky," Maisie whispered.

"So's just sitting here waiting. The drums mean something. I've got to find out what," Fargo said and moved to the door, dropped to the ground, and closed the door behind him. He began to crawl to the rear of the house; then flattening himself onto his stomach, he inched his way toward the line of trees. The moon stayed hidden behind scurrying clouds for most of the night, and he was grateful for that. Snakelike, he crawled toward the tree line, where he saw one Sioux leaning against the trunk of a young fir set back a few feet from the two Indians on either side of him.

Fargo continued to crawl along the ground, his eyes flickering to the Sioux on each side of him. One sat cross-legged on the ground, his eyes half-closed, the other standing a dozen feet away, his eyes on the house. Fargo crawled past both men on his way to the Indian leaning against the tree. The Sioux, while not asleep, was too relaxed to be alert, and Fargo was almost at his feet when he paused, every muscle in his body taut. He would have but one chance, he knew, and it had to be swift and silent. Borrowing from the Sioux's own stealthy methods, Fargo gathered himself, then propelled himself up and forward, his left hand outstretched and rigid as a board, slamming into the Indian's throat, while his right hand smashed the man's jaw sideways. Closing both hands, he snapped the Sioux's head half around.

The only sound was the almost inaudible breaking of neck bones.

He caught the man under his armpits before he fell and lowered him to the ground, silently pushing him into the sagebrush. Moving forward at a crouch, Fargo saw the pony a few feet away, took hold of the leather thong halter, and led the animal away, continuing until he was into the forest. Swinging up onto the pony's back, Fargo rode through the trees as he followed the sound of the drums, which hadn't let up for an instant. He had guessed right—the drums were almost a mile away. He slowed as they grew louder, until he saw the camp, a dozen tipis and a fire burning in the center. A line of bur oak afforded him the chance to move close, and he slid from the pony and crept almost to the edge of the camp. Dropping to one knee, he saw some thirty Sioux, braves and squaws, watching another dozen figures dancing around the fire, each costumed and masked.

The beat of the drums was unceasing, hypnotic, and he saw a central figure in a shaman's regalia, complete with medicine bundle. He chanted to the dancers' bobbing and weaving and raised his arms skyward to rattle long-necked gourds. Fargo caught the word *Wakantanka*, the Sioux term for the supernatural, the mysterious forces beyond man. He listened, straining his ears, and caught phrases from the masked dancers. His lips pulled back in a grimace. They were asking for help against the spirits of evil, calling on the shaman to invoke spells that would protect them in what they had to do. Damn, Fargo thought silently. They had decided they had to do battle against the evil spirits, a challenge that called for even greater protection than going to war against a mortal enemy.

But as he listened, straining his limited knowledge of Siouan, he managed to catch the warning the shaman gave to both dancers and onlookers. They were to be very careful not to come too close to the place of the evil spirits, or they would risk being swept up by their powers. The warning was given a number of times, along with chants and spells for protection and bravery. The dancers went on, replaced by new ones from time to time, and the drums never ceased. It would go on all night, he knew—not that morning was very far away. But he crawled back to where he'd left the Indian pony. He had learned all there was to learn. The Sioux were girding themselves to challenge the evil spirits, to someway, somehow, attempt to vanquish them or chase them away.

He wondered what they'd decide to do as he rode back toward the forest. They would not lack bravery. He knew the Sioux too well for that. And they were being given the added armor of the shaman's spells. But to challenge the spirits was an almost unheard of act of daring. They could fall back on a show of force, a mock attack calculated to show they had no fear and send the spirits fleeing. That would not be cowardice in their eyes. It would follow the shaman's warning and be a kind of coup. Or they might choose a half-dozen volunteers to penetrate the house and kill the humans who were by now possessed by evil spirits. That would slay two enemies at once and rid the house of the spirits. Fargo swore silently as he wondered what else they could do. The forest of giant fir trees loomed up in the last of the night.

He slowed the Indian pony as he rode through the trees and slid to the ground to proceed on foot as he neared the clearing. The Sioux were still silent and motionless as they stood guard around the house. They hadn't discovered the one he'd killed yet. Fargo dropped to the ground on his belly and began to crawl again. He passed the dead Sioux, inching his way between the other two Indians, and slowly crept along the cleared stretch of land. When he reached the house, the first faint tint of dawn was beginning to touch the far reaches of the sky, and he pushed his way inside and lay still for a long moment of thankfulness.

He rose to his feet finally and saw dawn spreading outside the window and heard the shuffle of footsteps from the other room. Marcy emerged first, hurried to him, and came into his arms. "Thank God you're back. I didn't sleep at all. I kept waiting and worrying," she said.

He glanced over her head and saw Maisie there. "Marcy's the sentimentalist," she said, a hint of disdain in her voice.

"You slept, I take it," Fargo said.

"Yes. I was sure you'd make it," Maisie said.

"Why?" Fargo asked.

"You want to make sure I'm going to keep our bargain," she said, cool amusement touching the even cooler blue eyes. He allowed a snort of wry agreement. "What did you find out?" she asked.

"They're working themselves up to do something. I wish I knew what," he said. "Which means we have to be ready for whatever it is. I want every door bolted and every window locked."

"When will they come?" Maisie asked.

"When the drums stop," Fargo said as the drums continued to pound in the distance.

"Then I resume searching for the will right now," she snapped, spinning to go into the next room.

"I'll see to the door and the windows," Fargo said as Marcy followed her sister. He found that most of the windows were fitted with locks, and the door had a strong bolt. When he finished he found Maisie in the large bedroom, the small handbag hanging from her shoulder as she searched the drawers of a dresser. She bent down and pulled open a bottom drawer, flinging shirts and socks out onto the floor. Suddenly she gave a half cry, half gasp and stood up, a long sheet of paper in her hand. A lighted lantern rested on the floor nearby.

"This is it," she said excitedly, and Marcy stepped closer. Fargo moved to stand beside her, where he could see over her shoulder. The will, written in a flowing hand, hardly filled half the piece of paper. Fargo heard Maisie's voice as he read alongside her.

Be it known hereby to all persons that I, Davis Kendrick, being of sound mind and disposition, having no heirs or relatives, and acting of my own free will, do hereby bequeath all of my worldly possessions and properties to my employee, Mr. Brad Kelly, of Redrock, Dakota territory, for his lifetime of faithful work. To this last will and testament, I affix my hand on this day of August 5, 1859.

Davis Kendrick

Maisie let a small sound escape her, and Fargo watched her rereading the will. "I'm sorry," he said. Maisie turned to him, her lips pursed. He felt the furrow dig into his brow as he saw her half shrug, a small, almost offhanded gesture. Maisie's even-featured face showed a quiet calm.

Only that—no anger, no shock, not even disappointment—only a wry smile.

"So much for that," she murmured.

"That's all?" Fargo asked, his frown deepening. "You were so sure your Pa's name was on that will."

"I was wrong," she said with another shrug.

Fargo felt himself staring at her, thoughts racing through his mind. "You're not surprised, are you?" he demanded. "Goddamn, you're not surprised at all."

She didn't answer, but moved to the kerosene lamp. Before he could stop her, she dropped the document into the open top of the lamp. It burst into instant flame and curled into ashes in seconds. Fargo stared, still contemplating the meaning of the thoughts that filled his mind when Maisie turned to walk past him. "There is no will now," she said. Moving past him, she brushed against one corner of the dresser and knocked the handbag from her shoulder. It fell to the floor, the contents spilling out.

He bent down to help pick them up and his eyes halted on an official-looking piece of paper. The words at the top leaped out at him as he picked it up:

LAND CLAIMS FORM—U.S. GOVERNMENT
DAKOTA TERRITORY

Fargo's eyes went down to the lines that followed and he read aloud. "Claim filed by Maisie Wilson for all the lands and properties belonging to Davis Kendrick, said lands and properties being unencumbered by any wills, testaments, or assignments, and therefore subject to all claims submitted in order of filing. Dated September 10, 1860, anno Domini."

Fargo's eyes went to Maisie, all the thoughts racing

through his mind finding dark confirmation. "You filled out this claim long ago. That means you were sure the will named Brad Kelly. You'd never have filled it out if you thought your Pa was on that will," he said.

Maisie's cold eyes didn't blink. "Pa was never strong enough. He was soft inside, like Marcy. No steel in him. Kendrick knew that. He'd never leave everything to Pa."

"You got Pa to go to Brad Kelly," Marcy cut in, astonishment in her voice. "What'd you tell him to make him do that?"

"I told Pa I knew Kendrick had put his name on the will and Brad Kelly was going to stop him from getting it," Maisie said.

"So he went to Brad Kelly angry enough to draw on him, only Kelly drew first," Fargo interrupted, and Maisie's cool silence was her answer. "Then you had to change plans fast," Fargo went on. "You had to make Brad Kelly into the villain and cast yourself as the daughter driven to revenge by grief. When I came into the picture you had me set that up for you. Everything you told me after that was a pack of lies, all that shit about having to find the will to prove your pa's name was on it—all a crock of shit. You had to find the will so you could destroy it and file the claim."

"Which is exactly what I'm going to do," Maisie said.

"You lied from the very start, to everybody, all so you could get your hands on Kendrick's land," Fargo said. "You are one rip-snorting, no-holds-barred little bitch," Fargo said. Unfortunately it sounded like a compliment, he realized, and knew that in a way it was exactly that.

He was still staring at Maisie, still sorting out the enormity of her Machiavellian maneuvers when Marcy's voice cut into his thoughts. "The drums have stopped," she said.

Fargo shook away his thoughts, and the silence suddenly seemed loud. He turned to stride from the room, the two young women on his heels. He opened the front door of the house. "You have guns?" he asked, and both nodded. "Get them," he said and went outside, where he took the rifle from the Ovaro and untethered the horses. When he went back inside and bolted the door, Maisie stood at one window, Marcy at another, each with a revolver in hand.

He stopped alongside Marcy and peered out at the treeline. He guessed they waited some twenty minutes before the new riders appeared, moving silently through the trees to join the others, who did not leave this time. Fargo unlatched the window and opened it enough for him and Marcy to kneel down and shoot without breaking the glass. Maisie did the same, he saw, and as he watched, the Sioux began to move forward just beyond the trees. They began to ride around the house, at a walk at first, then a trot, then a canter, and finally a gallop. They rode in a double line, those in front shouting and waving their bows, those in the second row holding their bows at their sides. He allowed himself to enjoy a moment of hope. Perhaps they were indeed going to keep their distance and put on a show to intimidate the evil spirits. He let the hope grow stronger as they made three circles around the house. Then suddenly a dozen in the second row spun their horses and broke away from the others to race toward the house.

He saw their bows drawn back and the flaming balls of rags and feathers that tipped each arrow. The first volley of fire arrows struck the side of the house as Fargo raised the rifle. "Shoot, goddammit," he shouted as he fired at one of the first wave of attackers, who had turned and were racing back to the trees while another dozen darted forward. The fire arrows imbedded themselves into the wood of the outer walls. Fargo's shots sent two of the Sioux toppling from their ponies as they raced back to the trees. But another band galloped toward the house, halted, and fired their fusillade of fire arrows. He saw that the arrows were being lighted by others on foot in the trees.

Maisie and Marcy were missing most of their shots, as the Sioux came only close enough to the house to release their fire arrows and race away. They had hit upon a way to destroy the place where the evil spirits dwelled and at the same time heed the shaman's warning of not getting too close. Fargo swore as he heard the thud of more arrows slamming into the rear and sides of the house and the odor of burning wood began to rise into the air. He got off a shot that sent one more attacker toppling from his pony, but only after the Indian had sent his arrow into the front door. The smell of burning wood grew stronger, and Fargo saw the tongues of flame licking at the corner of the house where the rounded spires rose.

"We'll have to try and run for it—get to the horses and run," Maisie said.

"You won't get fifty feet," Fargo said. "I want you to fire off another volley and then follow me." He raised the rifle and fired a fusillade at a half-dozen riders as they charged and whirled away. Two of his shots hit home and two of the ponies raced away riderless. "Come on," Fargo hissed at the two women as, staying low in a crouch, he ran from the window just as an arrow smashed through the glass. "Into the cellar," he ordered as he opened the cellar door. Maisie held back.

"We'll be trapped down there," she said.

"That's right, but it's also our only chance. It's got a good solid roof and stone walls and enough air," he said and stood back as Marcy went down the steps and Maisie followed. He went down last and pulled the door shut behind him. Marcy dropped to the cellar floor, fear wreathing her face as Maisie halted beside her.

"We just sit here and wait?" Maisie asked.

"You think we've a prayer of a chance to get through them outside?" Fargo returned, and her lips tightened.

"If we're not burned to death, we'll be smoked to death," Maisie said.

"Stone walls don't burn, and most of the smoke will rise," Fargo said.

"Did you have this figured out as our way to stay alive?" Marcy asked, and he allowed a grim smile.

"No, I wasn't that smart. This is strictly an on-the-spot, last-ditch move. I'd hoped they'd keep away or come in close for a regular attack. That way we'd have been able to pick off enough of them to maybe send them high-tailing it. They outsmarted me—but then they're not really attacking us."

"They're attacking the evil spirits and their home," Marcy said.

"Bull's-eye," Fargo said and ducked his head in an automatic reaction as the house shook with the collapse of a piece of wall. Stray tendrils of smoke sifted down into the cellar, and he could hear the crackle of flames overhead and feel the heat from above. Another beam fell and the cellar roof trembled. The smell of smoke was strong now, the sound of flames becoming a crackling roar. The house burned furiously above them, the fire devouring everything it could. The Sioux were watching from the tree line, he knew, certain the roaring fire was destroying the evil spirits, purifying the flesh and the spirit just as witches were once burned to erase all vestiges of evil.

Marcy sat with her arms clasped around herself, still holding the revolver in one hand, her eyes shut as if that would help shut out the sound and the odor. Maisie stood with her face expressionless, blue eyes hard as she listened. The cellar shook again and Fargo heard the crash of wood above. A sudden shower of sparks shot down the stairs as the cellar door collapsed. Marcy's eyes snapped open, fear stark in their dark depths. "Stay right where you are," Fargo said with quiet calm and watched a piece of burning wood fall halfway down the stairs. A puff of smoke swirled down from the steps and quickly dissipated. But the crackle of flame was less now. The house had been consumed; the fire was beginning to die without the fuel to keep it alive. But he heard another sound, harsh and scraping, and his eyes went to the cellar roof.

He flung himself into a dive and swept Marcy with him as pieces of stone crashed down, along with burning pieces of planking. Maisie had leaped to the side and avoided the debris, and Fargo saw her eyes find him as he still clutched Marcy. "You said the roof would hold," she accused.

"I thought it would. Sue me," he snapped and pushed to his feet. Two more pieces of board fell through the jagged hole to burn with a shower of sparks. Fargo peered up at the cellar ceiling and saw where two more beams lay burning across the hole. But the rest of the house no longer existed, he saw, the charred debris smoldering with little rivulets of flame. The smoke had grown denser but it spiraled up into the air. Fargo sat down against the far wall with Marcy.

"When do you figure they'll come searching what's left of the place?" Maisie asked from across the stones and simmering pieces of wood.

"I don't figure they'll come searching at all," Fargo said. "They'll expect nothing could've survived the fire. I'd expect pretty much the same if I was out there watching."

"How long do you think it'll be before we can leave here?" she asked.

"Not till the morning. It'll take overnight for things to cool down up there," Fargo answered.

"Maybe the Sioux will keep a watch through the morning," Marcy said.

"I wouldn't expect so," Fargo said and leaned back against the stone wall, feeling the radiating heat through his shirt. "They did what they came to do. They'll go back and celebrate. How they faced the place of the evil spirits and wiped it out will be a part of all their campfire stories from now on."

"They're not the only ones who'll celebrate," Maisie said as she settled herself against the opposite wall. Fargo remained silent as thoughts hung in his mind. He pushed them aside, knowing he'd have to deal with them soon enough. The last crackle of flame died away, and only the occasional hiss of a still-burning section of beam drifted down to the cellar. Finally, that too ceased, and there was only the silence and the sharp, acrid odor of smoke, charred wood, and blackened stone. Fargo stretched out on the cellar floor as the day wound to an end and the night brought darkness. The cellar became pitch-black and he took off his shirt, put it beneath his head, and prepared to sleep.

He heard Maisie moving, coming close and settling herself against the wall. Marcy lay motionless on the other side of him, her breathing a faint sighing sound. "I'm going to get some sleep. You two do the same," he said. He closed his eyes and had immersed himself in the darkness when suddenly he felt the hand touch his leg, moving to rest against his inner thigh. He hadn't a clue as to whose hand it was and knew he didn't dare whisper a name. He lay unmoving and finally the half-whispered words came. "I'll make it all up to you. I'll find a moment," Maisie's voice said.

Fargo said nothing. He felt her hand move up to curl itself around him through his Levi's, relax, and remain there. He heard Maisie's even breathing as she drew sleep around herself, her hand staying against him. He had just closed his eyes when he felt another hand touch his, then curl itself into a small fist inside his hand in the total blackness, a wordless message of its own. He finally slept, bothered because instead of a sense of anticipation, he had only a sense of foreboding.

9

He woke with the dawn and sat up as Maisie's hand fell away and Marcy's uncurled from inside his. He pushed to his feet, let them wake and rub sleep from their eyes while he stared up through the hole in the ceiling. Two beams that had fallen across it had burned themselves into charred pieces, and the acrid odor of burnt wood still hung in the air. He moved to the steps that led from the cellar, started to carefully climb them. The top three were partly burned, but with enough left to be usable. He climbed up to stand in the midst of what once had been a strange, malevolent house. It was only misshapen shards of charred lumber now, most of it reduced to cinders.

He moved through the fire-blackened remains, kicking aside a piece of wood here, an end of a beam there, and sending up little spirals of soot. He gazed out across the land to the tree line. Nothing moved, no silent forms standing watch. It was as he expected it would be. As Maisie and Marcy climbed out of the cellar, he stepped from what had been the main room of the house and whistled. He waited, whistled again, then again, and finally saw the flash of black forequarters and white midsection through the trees. The Ovaro trotted to him and put its head down to be nuzzled and stroked.

"I'll go see if I can round up some of the horses," Fargo said, swinging into the saddle and trotting into the forest. He found Maisie's big bay first, grazing a quarter-mile away, and then Marcy's mount and one of the pack-horses not far away. He hadn't expected they'd stray far and was grateful the Sioux hadn't taken them. Gathering the bay and the other two horses, he returned to the clearing and the charred circle of land in the center of it. Maisie stood outside the blackened remains—the hand-bag over her shoulder, he noted. The claim form was safely inside it, he knew, and felt the grimness settle over him at once. "Mount up and let's get out of here," he said. "You two take turns leading the packhorse."

He moved the Ovaro through the forest slowly, let the two women catch up to him, and then made a wide circle around the area of the Sioux camp. He found a stream hidden behind a rock formation of gray basalt, clusters of twisted hawthorn growing from the stone.

"I want to bathe. I smell of smoke and I'm covered with soot," Maisie said, halting and heading for the stream.

"Me, too," Marcy said and followed Maisie as both shed clothes at the edge of the stream behind a tall rock.

He listened to them splashing in the stream as he dis-mounted and crept to where Maisie's handbag lay where she'd let it fall. He opened it and removed the claim form. Putting the form in his pocket, he closed the hand-bag and left it where she'd dropped it. He climbed onto the rock and stood guard, his eyes sweeping the land. It was a simple precaution. There were other Sioux tribes that roamed the territory. But nothing moved, and when Maisie and Marcy finished and dried themselves on tow-els from their saddle packs, he went down to the stream, undressed, and washed, wishing he could wash away what lay inside him as easily as he had his outside.

He dried himself with his own towel, dressed, and found Marcy still brushing her hair while Maisie waited with faint impatience in her face. "We ride single file," he said as he led the way east. He sought narrow passages between rocks, and whatever stands of hackberry and bur oak he could find and traversed dry lake beds, staying on terrain that resisted showing hoofprints as much as he could. He set long, exhausting days that made both women eager to sleep each night. It was on the fourth night, under a full moon, that Maisie came to him. "I'd like to make a detour before we reach Redrock," she said. "It'd only take another half day."

"To the territory claims office?" Fargo smiled, and she nodded.

"I don't think so, honey," Fargo said and saw Marcy come closer out of the corner of his eye, a piece of jerky in one hand.

"I don't think that's your call, Fargo," Maisie said coolly.

"Well, I'm calling it, honey, just the way I'm taking you back to Sheriff Ludlow," he said.

"Of course we're going back to Ludlow. I'll clear you of everything, just the way I agreed to do," Maisie said, taking a step closer. "And I'll make it all up to you, as I promised. I just haven't found the moment yet."

"There's not going to be any moment. I'm clearing my name by taking you in for murder," Fargo said.

The blue eyes flashed fire instantly. "You out of your mind?" she threw back.

"Not anymore," Fargo said. "You murdered Brad Kelly. You knew he shot your pa in self-defense, yet you set him up so's you could kill him. Three of his men, too. Then you took those hired hands along to use as targets. That's another kind of murder. Though you didn't intend it, you're even responsible for getting your own pa killed. You engineered everything, and murder was at the center of all of it. You've got a lot of paying up to do, honey."

"Nobody's going to believe a word of any of this. Ludlow didn't believe you before. He's not going to believe you now. The Kelly brothers will remember it was you who went after them to keep them from following me."

"Ludlow will believe me this time. So will everyone else when they see this," Fargo said and drew the claim form from his pocket. He waved it at her for a moment and then returned it to his pocket. "It'll tie it all together for them just as it did for me," Fargo said.

Maisie's eyes were blue steel, the icy fury in her every feature. "Bastard," she hissed. "Stinking, rotten bastard."

"Bitch," he said. "Lying, stealing, murdering bitch." He glanced past her at Marcy, who watched, her dark eyes wide, full of pain and despair and a terrible sadness. Reaching forward quickly, he pulled the revolver from Maisie's waistband. "I'll just keep hold of this," he said.

Maisie spun on Marcy, fury in her voice. "You going to let him do this? I'm your sister, dammit," she spit out.

Marcy had only the terrible sadness in her eyes. "I know," she said. "And I'm so sorry for that."

"I should've known better than to depend on you for any guts," Maisie said, spun on her heel, and strode to the big bay.

"What are you doing?" Fargo asked.

"Getting my blanket," she said, reaching into her saddlebag. He turned his eyes on Marcy and felt terribly sorry for her. Maisie's voice cut into his thoughts as a steel blade cuts through grass. "Drop my gun. Then take your Colt out of its holster," she said. Fargo turned to see the pistol in her hand, a Remington four-barreled derringer with three-inch barrels and .32-caliber bullets. It fired the four barrels in succession and was a deadly little weapon.

He dropped her pistol to the ground and lifted the Colt from its holster and let it fall to the ground, aware that Maisie was a crack shot. He retreated a pace as she stepped forward and kicked the guns to one side. "I've been growing more and more afraid I'd misjudged you, and now I'm sure of it. You're as full of principles and conscience as a damn preacher."

"Hardly. I just have my limits," Fargo said, eyeing the derringer. But the deadly little gun didn't waver.

"You just reached them," Maisie said. "Dead men can't tell anyone anything."

"Maisie, no," Marcy's voice cut in. "You can't."

"Shut up and mind your own business," Maisie flung at her without taking her eyes from Fargo. "I'm not losing everything because of his conscience."

"You probably never intended to keep your part of our bargain, did you?" Fargo said to Maisie.

"It might have been awkward, all that convincing Ludlow. This way is much better. I'll explain how you were behind everything and I finally got a chance to break away from you." Maisie raised the derringer a fraction.

"No, you're not going to kill him," Marcy said, her voice rising. "Drop the gun, Maisie."

Fargo's eyes went to her. She had the revolver held

out with both hands, aimed at Maisie. He flicked a glance at Maisie and saw her throw Marcy a look of pure disdain. "Don't get in the way. You and I both know you won't use that," she said. "Now, put it down while I kill him."

"I'll use it," Marcy shouted, her voice breaking.

"No, you won't," Maisie uttered, and Fargo swore helplessly as he saw her cock the hammer on the derringer. His eyes were on her when the shot rang out and Maisie half spun, the red stain appearing as if by magic at her shoulder. The derringer fell from her grip as she staggered backward. Fargo rushed forward and scooped up the little revolver as Maisie sat down hard, one hand to her shoulder.

She stared at Marcy, shock filling her face, her eyes wide with astonishment. "No steel, you said?" Fargo slid at her. "Seems you were wrong." She continued to stare at Marcy in disbelief, and Fargo looked at Marcy and saw she still held the gun pointed with both hands, her arms still outstretched. He stepped forward, gently pried the revolver from her fingers, and held her as she sank to the ground, a deep sob tearing from insider her.

He returned to Maisie, who sat still in shock and looked at the spreading red stain. "Shoulder wound," he said. "I'll bandage it. The doc can treat it in Redrock." Maisie was silent as he tore the shirt from her shoulder and used part of another of her blouses from the saddle-bag to fashion a bandage. When he finished, he tied her to the trunk of a hawthorn as she glared at him.

"I'm shot. I can't run," she said.

"You just found out you should never underestimate anyone," Fargo said.

"Screw you," Maisie hissed as he left her. He lay

down with Marcy and she clung to him, even when she finally slept. When morning dawned he untied Maisie, changed her bandage, and helped her onto the big bay. He was about to climb onto the Ovaro when Marcy came to him.

"I didn't know I could do it," she said. "I'm not just soft inside."

"You found your steel. I'm just glad you picked that moment to find it," Fargo said, and she wrapped her arms around him for a moment.

"How touching," Maisie said as Marcy pulled back, ignoring her. Fargo led the way back, once again staying in protected passages until the terrain changed and he quickened the pace. It was late afternoon when they rode into Redrock and halted at the sheriff's office. Ludlow rose in astonishment, one leg still bandaged, and stared openmouthed at Fargo, then Maisie.

"Hear me out," Fargo said, dismounting and swinging Maisie from her horse. He spoke quickly, leaving out nothing. It was the claim form that tied all his explanations together, as he knew it would. When he finished, the sheriff put wrist irons on Maisie before her trip to the doctor.

"I'll be taking no chances with you, Maisie Wilson," he said. Maisie paused before Marcy and Fargo as a deputy started to lead her away, disdain in her blue eyes as they bored into Marcy.

"You surprised me, little sister," she said. "But it was a once-in-a-lifetime thing. You're still soft inside. You could never do it again."

Marcy's voice was quietly cold. "He laid me first. You were an afterthought, second choice," she said. Maisie's scream of rage split the air as she lunged at Marcy. The deputy pulled her back, and she was still screaming as he led her away. Fargo met Marcy's eyes and saw the triumph in them. "I guess there are all sorts of ways to use steel once you find it," she said.

"All sorts of ways," he echoed.

"And all sorts of ways to make love."

"All sorts of ways."

Marcy's arms slid around his neck, the deep breasts soft against his chest. "Show me," she murmured.

"It's a deal," he said.

"Anywhere, everywhere, except one thing—no weird, crazy house," she said.

"Only weird, crazy positions," he said, and she nodded happily against him. This would be a fire he'd enjoy, he told himself as they rode off.

LOOKING FORWARD!
The following is the opening
section from the next novel in the exciting
Trailsman series from Signet:

THE TRAILSMAN #166
BLACK MESA TREACHERY

The high plateau near Santa Fe, 1860,
a harsh land of red rock and rolling thunder,
where some men find the face of God
and others do the devil's work . . .

"You Skye Fargo?"

The tall man with the lake-blue eyes glanced up from his whiskey at the rotund bartender. Another man standing nearby, foot hooked over the bar rail and beer in hand, nudged his companion, and the two of them gawked at the tall stranger.

"Did you hear that? That's Skye Fargo," one of them whispered to the other. "They call him the Trailsman. I heard all about him."

"Yeah—me, too," the other whispered back, awe in his voice. "Wonder what he's doing down here in Taos."

Skye Fargo nodded once to the bartender, paying no attention to the two men.

"Forgot to tell you earlier when you came in, Mister

Fargo. Got a message for you," the bartender said, handing him a folded paper.

Fargo took it and pushed his empty glass across the bar. As it was being refilled, he examined the writing on the front—his name in bold black letters—and the large wax seal on the back with its crucifix, initialed A and F. Yeah, it was the message he'd been waiting for all afternoon. He glared at the bartender, suspecting him of holding the letter back in order to sell a few more drinks. As he broke the seal, Fargo gazed around the half-deserted bar. Late-afternoon sun poured in past the bat wing doors. In a dark corner, four men were playing a deadly earnest game of poker, as they had been all afternoon. A dove in a faded green dress was talking to a heavyset fellow, a rancher by the looks of him. And then there were the two men—cowpoke types—staring at his every move. Fargo turned away from them and opened the paper.

Meet him at Castle Rock on the Thunder Trail, edge of Tewa land. At moonrise. Bring him to Chimayò. Meanwhile, travel incognito—danger everywhere. Go with God. Amado Fernandez.

Moonrise. Hell, that was around midnight. Fargo glanced at the golden light across the warped board floor. It was getting on to sunset. He'd never make it in time. It was at least five or six hours of fast riding to the rendezvous point. Hastily, he pulled a couple of coins out of his pocket, threw them on the counter, and turned to go.

"Hey! Hey!" one of the cowpokes called after him as he headed toward the door. "Ain't you Skye Fargo?

Ain't you the Trailsman?" The men at the poker table lowered their cards and craned their necks to stare at him. Then a couple of them pointed at him and muttered to one another. Fargo ignored them all and pushed through the doors. Great. Everybody in the Taos barroom had got a good look at him. And the message had said to travel incognito. Well, at least he'd be out of town in no time.

At the stable, he asked for the Ovaro and the stable-boy brought it out. The pinto's black-and-white coat gleamed magnificently in the slanting light. It nuzzled Fargo.

"Beautiful horse you got here, Mister Fargo," the boy said, stroking the pinto's neck, reluctant to let go of the reins. Fargo mounted. The pinto moved restlessly under him, eager to be away on the trail.

"You're awful popular, Mister Fargo," the boy said.

"What do you mean?"

"Those two guys looking for you," the kid said. "I told them you were over at the hotel. Didn't they find you?"

"Two guys? What did they look like?"

The boy screwed up his face, remembering.

"The first was one of them Catholic padres. Came in on a donkey around midday. Said he had some letter for you." Fargo nodded, saying nothing. Yes, the brother who had brought the message from Padre Amado Fernandez. "And then just a quarter-hour ago. Big fellow. Tall and all dressed in black. Smartlike. Riding a chestnut. I asked if he didn't want to stable her, but he said he was in a hurry to find you. Was in an awful bad mood."

153

Fargo sat for a moment in thought. Who was the man in black who had followed him to Taos? Sounded like trouble for sure. Meanwhile, the sun was dropping swiftly over the distant mountain, staining the clouds blood-red. There was no time to lose, no time to find out what trouble was after him. Fargo pulled a coin out of his pocket and flipped it to the kid.

"Tell him you found out I was heading due north, up to Ute country."

"Sure. Sure, Mister Fargo."

Fargo headed out, riding through the back streets toward the head of the trail that led south out of Taos. But curiosity got the better of him. Who the hell was on his tail? He decided to have a quick look and turned back into an alley that led toward the main square. He dismounted and walked forward to stand beside a storefront where he was out of sight but had a good view.

All around the square, bars were just starting to heat up for the night. The strains of a honky-tonk piano floated on the air and several knots of men came into sight, swaggering in different directions toward the various watering holes. A line of horses was hitched in front of the Taos Hotel. Among them stood a glistening black-pointed chestnut. As Fargo watched, a tall, broad-shouldered man dressed all in black came out of the front door. Even from a distance, Fargo's keen gaze could discern his broken nose and his glittering black eyes. The tall man paused for a moment, looked up and down the square, and then stepped down the stairs, heading for one of the bars. Just then, Fargo spotted the stableboy running up the dusty street in pursuit, to tell the stranger that he had headed north. Fargo didn't wait but turned back, mounted the pinto, and galloped out of town.

Who the hell was the big man? He'd never seen him before. But he could have been sent by any one of a hundred men who had reason to hunt him down, thought Fargo. If a man lived hard and fast, he made a lot of friends and an equal number of enemies. Anyway, the kid would throw the stranger off his scent. There was no time to deal with him now.

The pinto's powerful legs pounded the trail as they climbed the hill. Soon, the town of Taos lay behind them, a clutter of board and adobe buildings on the sage plain at the foot of the high snowy peaks to the east. West of town, the sage plain stretched for miles toward the mountains at the horizon. As he gained the crest of the hill and the sage plain fell away below, Fargo spotted the dark, jagged line of the gorge where the mighty Rio Grande cut deep into the earth.

But right now, his business lay to the south, and as they came over the top of the hill, Taos disappeared from view and Fargo's thoughts turned to what lay ahead. It had been a week since the first message had come from Padre Amado Fernandez. Fargo had met the priest years before at a mission in California. Fernandez had struck him as one of the few holy men who seemed to have his feet on the ground. In his California parish, the priest had built an orphanage and a hospital, and then got the whole town reorganized after it had been burnt to the ground by a raging brushfire. He'd had one of the most successful missions in the whole country. Then the local archbishop transferred him down to the Chimayò Mission near Santa Fe. That had been five years ago, and Fargo hadn't heard a word about Amado Fernandez since.

Then, the week before, a letter found him up in Kansas. The padre wrote that he needed Fargo's help. The instructions were to go to Taos and wait at the bar for a message. Fargo wondered what kind of trouble the padre could have got himself into. And who it was he was supposed to be meeting at Castle Rock. Well, he'd find all that out soon enough.

The sunset colors were fading in the west, and ahead of him the first star appeared over the southern horizon, which was sharp with buttes. The trail arched over the hills, curved through the dense and fragrant piñons, then descended toward the rocky, open land.

The rendezvous point—Thunder Trail and Castle Rock—were near Black Mesa. Fargo knew the mesa, a mammoth hulk of rock and earth with sheer cliffs rising straight up from the flat land below. Black Mesa could be seen for hundreds of miles around. But no matter how sunny the day, Black Mesa always seemed to be in shadow, and now, with the light fading steadily, it was a darker shadow in the shade of the mountains to the west. He headed toward the spot, the pinto galloping full out on the hard-packed trail. No time to lose. There was a good five hours to get to Castle Rock. And by then the moon would be up. He was going to be late. Whoever he was supposed to be meeting there would just have to wait.

The moon was a bright silver coin high in the black heavens. Fargo stood and stretched his limbs, then leaned against the night-cold stone in the shadow of Castle Rock. All around him, the nubby sage was like a woolen blanket folded over the hills. A few miles away, the huge dark shape of Black Mesa blocked out the stars in the sky. Fargo listened to the coyotes singing and the whir of bats and owls as they hunted. No one had come. He'd arrived about an hour after moonrise and had been waiting a good two hours more.

Fargo pulled up the collar of his buckskin jacket as the desert wind turned colder. Whoever it was had either given up on him before he'd arrived or wasn't going to show. He was just beginning to wonder if he ought to ride on to Chimayò when he saw it.

Movement. In the brush at the top of the hill. The Ovaro, hidden in the shadow of the rock, pawed nervously. Its keen nostrils had picked up the scent of something coming.

Yes, movement above on the hill. A figure walking in the brush. Then two, three. Fargo slid the Colt from its holster and the moonlight gleamed blue on the barrel. There was a long, wavering line of dark figures walking through sage, spread out across the hill as if searching, their heads bent low. As they came nearer, Fargo saw that they were all robed and hooded. Monks. He felt relief wash over him. He holstered his pistol and walked out to meet them.

His boots crunched on the gravel trail and the line came to a halt. Fargo raised a hand in greeting as he neared.

"What are you looking for?" he called out.

There was a long silence, and then one of the monks

stepped forward, his face hidden in the shadow beneath his cowl.

"Who are you?" the monk said gruffly.

Fargo suddenly felt a sensation of danger. Something was wrong. He must be on his guard, his instincts told him. Fargo didn't hesitate a second.

"Name's Brent Barker, Father," Fargo said in a loud and friendly voice. He kept his head down under his low hat brim, his face hidden from the glare of moonlight. "Heading down to Santa Fe. I think I took a wrong turn. I'd be much obliged if you could tell me which way it is."

The monks stood in silence for a long moment. Then the rough voice answered him again.

"Turn around, stranger," the monk said. "Santa Fe's over that way. About fifteen miles." He pointed across the broken land toward the southeast.

"Thank you kindly," Fargo said, backing away. "Since it's so late, I guess I'll just camp here for the night and head out there in the morning." Maybe whoever was supposed to meet him might still be coming.

"This is Tewa land," the monk said, his thick voice hard-edged. "And we've had some trouble out here. We don't like trespassers."

"Really?" Fargo said, keeping up the ruse of naïveté. "I heard of the Tewa tribe. Now, are *you* Tewa?"

"This is Tewa land," the monk repeated sternly. Fargo saw the glint of a rifle emerge from the folds of the dark robe. "And we are from the Tewa mission."

"I guess so," Fargo said. He returned to the shadow of Castle Rock and mounted the Ovaro. As he rode off, he turned and looked back. The dark figures of the monks still stood ranged across the hillside, watching him ride off. Who ever heard of a monk toting a rifle? He wondered what connection they had with the stranger he was supposed to have met at Castle Rock. Maybe he could get that question answered by Padre Amado Fernandez at Chimayò.

He had gone scarcely a mile and was just galloping up out of a shallow arroyo when the Ovaro shied and nickered. Fargo knew the signal. The pinto sensed something out there in the darkness. Something that didn't belong. Fargo reined in and sat for a long moment looking about him, his senses alert. The pinto moved nervously under him. Then he heard a sound, so faint another man would have missed it.

Fargo dismounted, drew his Colt, and made his way through the brush and pale, summer-dry grass. He heard the sound again. Unmistakable. A human noise, a moan. An instant later, he glimpsed a dark form. A man. Fargo glanced around, then bent over and turned him face up.

He was wearing a monk's robe. The moonlight fell across the face, which was badly disfigured. The nose had been smashed and the cheeks cut deep. Blood blackened his features so that Fargo could barely distinguish his face. The man tried to open his eyes and finally managed it. His lips parted, blood ran from his mouth, and Fargo heard the terrible moan again. Then he realized the man's tongue had been cut out.

"Take it easy," Fargo said, wondering if there was any chance this was the man he was supposed to meet. He propped him against a rock. He didn't have long to live, that was certain. There was nothing Fargo could do for him. Not even a drink of water would ease his suffering now.

"Who did this to you?" Fargo asked.

The man moaned and moved his head from side to side. Fargo felt his frustration. How could he communicate?

"I came to Castle Rock tonight to meet somebody," Fargo tried again. "Padre Amado Fernandez sent me."

At the padre's name, the man's eyes fluttered again and then fixed on Fargo's face with a look that was indecipherable. His hand stirred against Fargo and he moaned again. Fargo felt the man trying to press something into his hand and Fargo took it, then held it out in the moonlight. It was a length of rope, knotted many times.

"Is this a message?" Fargo asked. "For Amado Fernandez?" The dying man nodded slowly. His breath was strained now, rasping, and he brought his hands together, working. Fargo saw that he was trying to get his ring off his finger. He bent down and removed the ring. Then the man's hand scrabbled at the soil and came up with a handful of it, pressed it into Fargo's hand. He breathed once heavily and then no more.

Fargo felt the dry earth trickling through his fingers as he looked down at the dead man. Then a sound came from the top of the hill. He glanced up to see the line of monks coming silently down the slope. Swiftly, Fargo melted into the shadow of the nearby cutbank and pulled the Ovaro with him into the cover of the thick brush. A few minutes later, he heard the sounds of the approaching men.

"Over here!" one shouted. Fargo peered out from the brush and saw the dark shapes of the robed monks gathering around the dead man. They did not speak. They hoisted the corpse on their shoulders and then moved off again. Fargo watched as the silent procession disappeared over the hill.

What the hell was going on? Fargo wondered about the strange monk with the rifle who had warned him off the Tewa land. The monks had been searching for the one who'd been tortured. To rescue him or to kill him? It had been impossible to tell. Maybe Amado Fernandez would have some answers. Fargo rode off into the night.

Dawn was primrose-yellow as he reined in the Ovaro and sat looking down at the Sanctuario de Chimayò. All around, red rocks rose in weird formations. Here and there, stark black forms of rude wooden crosses marked the bare hillsides. Below, in the center of a small cluster of adobe buildings, stood the famous mission, its dun-colored walls softened by time and weather. Chickens scratched in the dust before the church. As he watched, a young boy ran across the yard and disappeared inside. The rusted iron bell in the tower began to move back and forth slowly and then pealed as the clapper hit the lip. The ringing sound, hollow in the cool morning air, resounded off the rocks. The doors to the nearby houses opened one by one, and rebozo-wrapped women and men in colorful cotton shirts headed toward the mission. When Fargo reached the churchyard, he dismounted. Through the open doors, he could hear the voice of Padre Amado intoning a sermon.

Fargo spotted a trough and pump and led the Ovaro over to it. After the horse drank its fill, Fargo led it into the stable nearby. He filled a manger with fresh oats, found curry combs, and gave the horse a thorough brush-down while it munched at the feed. He had just finished and was closing the stall door behind him when he heard Padre Amado's voice.

"Fargo! You're here! I was getting worried."

Padre Amado Fernandez had changed in the five years since Fargo had last met up with him. Amado's thick, wavy hair was grayer, the lines in his face etched more deeply, and his shoulders were stooped. And there was a sadness about him that Fargo had not seen before. The padre clapped him on the back.

"You didn't come in to hear my sermon?" Amado's old twinkle was in his kindly brown eyes.

"I'm just not the praying kind," Fargo said.

"You never have been," the padre said with a laugh. "Don't ever tell the archbishop I said this, but sometimes I think some men don't have to be." Then the padre's face grew serious and he looked around, concern in his face.

"But where is Lucero? Did you bring him to me? Did you get my message?"

"Yeah," Fargo said. Just then a flock of children came running up and surrounded Amado. They hopped up and down around him and tugged on his robe.

"Not now! Not now, my children," the padre said, swatting them gently away. Laughing and chattering like a flock of birds, the children ran off toward the parish garden. "Come inside and we will talk," Amado said.

The padre led the way past the small walled vegetable garden and through a narrow gate. They crossed a courtyard and entered a low door. Fargo found himself inside a simple whitewashed room. On one wall was a low rope bed with a blanket folded on one end. Above it hung a crucifix. On the other wall was a bench and a table. A carved wooden chair stood toward the center of the room. "Please," Padre Fernandez said, gesturing toward the chair as he seated himself on the bench. Fargo realized this was the padre's living apartment.

Amado Fernandez stared at the bare wall as Fargo told him about receiving the message in Taos and about the missed meeting at Castle Rock. His face took on a puzzled look when Fargo described the monks and the rifle he had glimpsed. When Fargo reached the part about finding the dying man, he retrieved the knotted rope and the ring from his pocket and handed them over. The padre took them and tears came to his eyes.

"This was Lucero's ring," he said, holding it up. "You see my initials here and the holy insignia. It was my ring and I gave it to him as a token of our friendship. Lucero said he would never take it off until he died."

"Who was this Lucero?"

"His given name was Dawn Mountain," Amado said. "He is . . . *was* chief of the Tewa."

"Tewa? But he was dressed like a monk."

"Yes. That part of your story is a great mystery to me," the padre said as he shook his head. "Lucero was a good Catholic, of course. But he was also a good Tewa. I know he continued to worship his Tewa gods, too, and—don't tell the archbishop this, either—I did not condemn him or his people for that. But why he would be dressed as a monk—I just don't understand this."

"Maybe it wasn't Lucero after all. Maybe Lucero is still alive."

"No, I am certain it was Lucero," Amado said, shaking his head sadly. "Because of this—" he held the ring aloft—"and because of what Lucero had told me. A month ago he came to tell me that there was bad medicine at the Tewa pueblo, but he could not explain what he meant. Then he sent a message. Find someone to help, it said. Send him to me at moonrise and I will have the information about the danger." The padre paused and wiped his face anxiously. He held the knotted rope aloft and stared at it, his brow furrowed with thought. "And now this is our only clue."

"It's some kind of signal," Fargo said. "Maybe how many knots there are. Looks like six."

"Yes, six," Amado said, twisting the cord slowly. "A knotted rope. This makes me think of something else, but I cannot remember what. I must meditate on this."

"And what about those monks?" Fargo asked.

A dark cloud passed over the padre's face. He rose and paced up and down on the stone floor and finally spoke.

"I am guilty of the sin of envy," the padre said, a touch of anger in his voice. "Envy! The basest of emotions. And so it is difficult for me to speak of this new mission that has come to the Tewa just three months ago. Their leader is Claudio Gonzalez. I had never heard of him, but he appeared one day, sent by the bishops in Mexico, and set up a mission near Black Mesa."

"What's he like?"

"A powerful man," the padre said. "As was my custom on Wednesdays, I rode my burro up to the Tewa pueblo the week he arrived. I introduced myself to the brothers, and they kept me waiting for an hour until he had time to see me. Then they ushered me into the small chapel there—the chapel where I have always made the communion! There he sat by the altar. He is very quiet and he keeps his hood on at all times. He motioned me to come forward and take communion from him, which I did. I could hardly see his face, but what I saw was badly scarred, as if he had suffered some terrible trial. He asked me questions about everyone in the territory. And when he spoke, his voice was like the voice of God."

Fargo watched as the padre paced the room again, his hands twisting the length of knotted rope that he held. He was obviously fighting his emotions.

"What did he say?"

"Only that he had been called to minister to the Tewa flock," Padre Amado said. "He blessed me and told me that God would send me a vision. I felt his holy power, as if I were in the presence of God himself. And then the room began to . . . well, to change. And I saw snakes coming up from the floor." The padre paused and his eyes took on a faraway look of remembrance. "I have never told anyone this before. Not even my own confessor. Somehow I found myself on my burrow going back to Chimayò, and the way was filled with snakes. Everywhere. I knew it was a message from God. And I knew that I had failed. That these were the creatures of my envy, of my ambition, of my own weakness."

The padre hung his head.

"I think there's a rational explanation for this," Fargo said. "Those snakes were just your imagination. Maybe you were just tired."

"No," the padre said. "It was a mystical experience. I

saw them, I tell you. And Gonzalez had told me I would have a vision from God. You see, he was right."

"I don't accept that," Fargo snapped.

"God has even taken my Tewa away," the padre added. "They do not come to Chimayò anymore. Not just at Black Mesa pueblo, but at the pueblos all around. They go to hear Gonzalez. He has many brothers to help him. His mission is now the most powerful in the territory."

"So who murdered Lucero?" Fargo asked.

"Maybe a Tewa," the padre said sadly. "Somebody jealous. Maybe Lucero had joined the brothers, and one of the Tewa felt betrayed and was threatening him."

"If that was the case, then Padre Gonzalez would have been able to stop it. And Lucero would have gone to him for help. I think this Padre Gonzalez wanted to keep Lucero quiet about something."

"Oh, certainly not!" Padre Amado said, his brows raised. "You will know when you meet him. Padre Gonzalez is a man of the cloth. He has taken holy vows. He is sacrificing his life to bring the word of God to this desert. No, I am certain that the brothers are not involved in this affair. Besides, you yourself saw them looking for poor Lucero's body. No, I am certain there is some other answer to this murder."

"Then why are the monks carrying rifles?"

Padre Amado paused for a moment. "Yes, that is very strange," he agreed. "But maybe they are in danger, too. If the brothers are carrying rifles, there must be a good reason. I am sure they would not use them to kill, but only to frighten away whatever danger was near. Like whoever killed Lucero."

Fargo felt certain the padre was just being naive.

"Maybe we should go up there and have a talk with Gonzalez," Fargo suggested.

"No, I cannot do that," Amado said sadly. "I am no longer welcome on the Tewa land. The tribe does not welcome me. They listen only to Padre Gonzalez. They have asked me to stay away. All except Lucero. Oh, maybe it is just my jealousy. Maybe I was wrong to call on you."

"No," Fargo said. "You're too hard on yourself, Padre. And this whole Gonzalez thing stinks."

The priest looked at him with surprise, and then with a glimmer of hope in his eyes. He shook his head again.

"Let us speak no more of it," he said. "You will rest today, and tonight we will dine together. My ward, Desideria, will join us tonight. She is in the convent at Santa Fe, and when she heard you were coming she was most eager to meet you." There was a twinkle in the padre's eyes.

Fargo rose, suddenly realizing how tired he was from the long night in the saddle. They made their way to the guest quarters, where the padre showed Fargo his room then left to attend to the business of the mission.

The guest quarters were better appointed than the padre's bare cell. A comfortable feather bed was covered with crisp white sheets and colorful blankets. A china washstand, leather chairs, and a tall wooden chifforobe filled the room. Fargo brought his gear in from the stable, pulled off his boots, and lay down. Sleep came fast, and his dreams were filled with the forms of monks and a writhing snake that turned into a knotted rope—which untied itself, knot by knot.

Fargo awoke in late afternoon and found a small cold

meal of tortillas and beans waiting for him on a tray. He ate, bathed, and walked outside. In the bare yard, the chickens were pecking. Three barefoot boys were propped against a cottonwood tree, dozing in the dappled shade. The iron bell was silent in the adobe tower. Fargo walked through the large wooden doors into the moist coolness of the sanctuary. On the dirt floor were rows of rude benches. Flickering candles lit the colorful pictures of saints in niches along the walls. Behind the simple cross at the altar was a carved wooden screen painted with images of birds and animals and flowers. A few people sat silently praying. Fargo heard the padre's voice and followed the sound into the room adjoining the sanctuary.

There Padre Amado was kneeling beside an old woman, binding her ankle with a bandage. Crutches and canes of various sizes and shapes were leaning against the walls all around the room. The padre looked up when Fargo entered.

"You see all the many people who have been healed here," the padre said, gesturing at the abandoned crutches. He finished binding the woman's ankle, got to his feet, fished around in his pocket, and then handed her a small packet. "Take these pills twice a day. And do not walk too much, senora. And pray. I am sure our Holy Father will make it better." The woman kissed the padre's hand and limped out of the room.

"Looks to me like you're the one making it better, Fargo said.

"A little medicine and a little faith work hand in hand," Padre Amado said. He glanced around the empty room, then picked up a bucket of earth that stood in a corner. "Come with me," he said and led the way to a small room toward the back. "Please stand at the door and tell me if anyone is coming."

Fargo did as he was told and then watched the padre kneel beside a small hole in the center of the dirt floor. He made the sign of the cross and then began carefully pouring the earth into the cavity.

"What are you doing?" Fargo asked.

"It is the healing mud," the padre explained as he worked. "Long ago, there was a spring on this place where the Indians came for healing. Then when the mission was built, people still came to take away a little of the moist earth for its curative properties. Only problem is, so many people come now that I must always put some more earth here, or the whole floor would soon disappear."

Fargo heard some voices and alerted the padre, who quickly secreted the empty bucket, rose, blessed the room again, and dusted off his hands as they left. A family of four passed them and nodded to the padre as they made their way toward the small room. Once outside, the padre walked around the yard.

"Maybe you think it is wrong of me to put this earth back? Maybe you think I am fooling the people?" the padre said distractedly.

"I think bandaging that woman's leg does more good than some holy mud," Fargo said.

"But sometimes medicine fails," the padre said. "And that is when people need something to believe in."

"Yeah, but other times people just think that believing will make everything come out all right. And then they don't act."

"Yes, Skye," the padre said with a laugh. "This is the difference between us. I am a man of faith. You are a man of action. Both of us righteous in our own ways."

The sound of approaching horses drew their attention. The padre's face brightened.

"That must be Desideria!" he said, his lined face wreathed in smiles. "The convent school has not allowed her to visit me at home for the last year. They are too strict, I think. So every week I go to see her in Santa Fe."

They watched as two palominos cantered toward them down the dusty road. Fargo made out the figures of two women as they came nearer and headed into the yard. The younger one, in a dark riding cape, reined in and jumped down from her horse. She came flying across the yard and embraced the padre. Behind her, the other woman, thin-faced and sallow and in a nun's habit, dismounted slowly.

"Father!" the young woman said. "I am so glad to be home!" She took a step back from him and then turned to face the mission church. "Oh, I have missed Chimayò!" She whirled about suddenly and regarded Fargo. Her dark eyes flashed. She was beautiful, honey-skinned with thick, waving hair that fell to her waist and large black eyes that sparkled with intelligence and humor. As she gazed at him, she unbuttoned her cape and slid it off her shoulders and he noticed her slender waist, the full curves of her hips, and beneath her white blouse, the blooming fullness of her breasts. He raised his eyes to hers again and saw her blush.

Padre Amado cleared his throat.

"This is Skye Fargo," he said. "My ward, Desideria Fernandez y Aznar."

The young woman extended her hand to him, a grave look on her face but merriment in her eyes.

"I have heard all about you, Mr. Trailsman," Desideria said. "All the girls at the convent . . . "

"That is quite enough, Desideria," the nun cut in, hurrying forward. She slapped the young woman's hand away from Fargo's. "I am Sister Alva. From the convent school at Santa Fe. I am responsible for the señorita." Sister Alva glowered at Fargo with an expression that left no doubt in his mind what she meant. He noticed that Desideria turned away to suppress a giggle.

"Come in, Sister Alva," the padre said, trying to take her arm. "We'll leave the young people here. Let me show you to your quarters. You must be tired after your journey."

Sister Alva shook off his arm and resolutely took Desideria's arm, pulling her along.

"Yes, you can show *us* where we are sleeping tonight."

The padre shrugged and followed the two women. Desideria looked back and smiled at Fargo as he followed them all inside.

"This mission is a failure," Sister Alva said. "Everyone in Santa Fe knows that. Why, you hardly have enough money for the candles. And from what I hear, nobody comes here anymore."

Padre Amado Fernandez put down his fork, picked up the wine bottle, and poured himself a glass, his hand trembling slightly. Desideria looked down at her plate, her cheeks flushed red.

"I suppose you are going to tell me I ought to be more like Padre Gonzalez over at Black Mesa," the padre said.

"Exactly," Sister Alva responded. "Why, he's got great plans for the whole territory. He came to call on the Mother Superior just two weeks ago. I think he's come up with new ideas for the convent, too. Then he gave a sermon to the young ladies. Stupendous! Simply stupendous! A voice like thunder!"

"What did you think?" Fargo asked Desideria quietly.

The young woman shrugged and glanced guiltily over toward her guardian. Clearly, she also had been impressed with Padre Gonzalez, but her loyalty kept her from admitting it.

"*And*," Sister Alva said importantly, "Padre Gonzalez has a direct connection to . . . " She paused dramatically. "To Rome! Straight to the Pope! He showed Mother Superior a letter right from the Vatican! Can you imagine? Gonzalez knows the Pope. And he's right here in our territory. I tell you, Gonzalez is a godsend."

"Just what are they teaching you in that convent?" Fargo broke in. He was tired of Sister Alva's worshipful praise of Gonzalez.

"In the mornings, Sister Margarita teaches us history and reading," Desideria said, flashing a smile at him. "Then Sister Gracia takes us outside and we learn about plants and animals, the sun and the stars. In the afternoons, we sew."

"And what about catechism?" Sister Alva asked sharply.

"Oh, yes," Desideria said. "Sister Alva teaches us religion." Desideria paused, her dark eyes on him. "But I read everything I can," she said with a rush. "I so want to understand the world. I want to know everything and to learn what is out there. I want—"

"That is quite enough, Desideria," Sister Alva cut in. "It is not correct for a girl to have so many wants. You must do as the saints do and curb your desires. Remember the tree of knowledge in the Garden of Eden."

Desideria fell silent, but Fargo could see the anger blazing in her eyes. She had a hot temper barely held in check. But he had always liked women with spirit. Sister Alva turned toward Padre Fernandez and began to talk about Gonzalez. Fargo reached under the table and lightly touched Desideria's knee. She started, then smiled and reached under the table to clasp his hand, entwining her warm fingers in his.

"More wine?" Fargo asked, filling her glass with his free hand. The padre and Sister Alva were engrossed in church gossip.

"I want to learn everything," Desideria said in a low voice. "You understand? Everything."

Under the table, she pulled his hand upward along her thigh until he felt her pressing her fingers against the bunched skirt between her legs.

"It is time we had our evening prayers, Desideria," Sister Alva announced, suddenly rising. Reluctantly, Desideria let go of his hand. Fargo rose as the two women left the room, then sat down again.

Padre Fernandez gazed after them, his face flushed.

"My Desideria will never be a nun," he said. "Not in a hundred years. Don't tell the archbishop I said this, but if every woman was a nun, there would be no more

Catholics." He chuckled and unsteadily poured himself another glass of wine, spilling some on the table. Fargo saw that the padre, probably depressed by all the talk about Gonzalez, had had too much to drink. He suggested they turn in and then helped the padre to his room.

"Maybe Sister Alva is right," Fernandez muttered as he staggered down the hall and then tripped. Fargo caught him and kept him from falling. "Maybe I am all washed up. Maybe God is trying to tell me that. I've sinned. Yes, I've sinned the sin of envy, and this is my punishment."

After he left the padre, Fargo let himself into his room. The evening was chilly, and he lit a fire in the round brick fireplace in one corner. Golden light flickered on the white walls. Fargo kicked off his boots and stripped off his shirt. He heard the creak of a door and the soft patter of feet on the stone floor of the hall. A moment later, his door was pushed open a few inches. The firelight caught the figure of Desideria clothed in a loose white gown, her long hair hanging down around her like a dark shawl.

"At the convent, all the girls tell stories about you, Skye Fargo," Desideria said shyly. "Everyone knows about you. They say you know everything about love. And I want to learn. I want to know everything. Will you teach me?"